The Unknown Among Us

The Unknown Among Us

Almondyne Petersson

Library of Congress Control Number:		2019917157
ISBN:	Hardcover	978-1-7960-6763-7
	Softcover	978-1-7960-6762-0
	eBook	978-1-7960-6761-3

Print information available on the last page.

Rev. date: 10/24/2019

To order additional copies of this book, contact:
Xlibris
1-888-795-4274
www.Xlibris.com
Orders@Xlibris.com
791411

PROLOGUE

The wind was cold and the rain was so loud against the shingles on the roof that it was the only thing to be heard at the dead of night, except for the crying. It seemed to be so loud that it blocked out the sound of the wind and rain. He stood there, his face covered by the hood of his long coat, listening to the crying inside the rundown cottage. The windows were all broken, the front door was broken down, not a single light around him or the cottage.

Wolves howled in the distance, maybe it was time for him to leave? But the crying kept his attention and perhaps his life would have turned out differently if he did turn and walk away. Who knows, maybe his life would have been filled with riches if he had just left. It was a thought that had crossed his mind many times after this night, how much different his life would be if he had turned and left, but he couldn't go back in time to stop himself from walking into that broken down cottage.

The soggy ground squished under his boots as he walked towards the cottage, the moonlight offered little light between the stormy clouds. He paused for a moment by the wooden steps, listening for any sounds of life other than the crying but all he heard were the wolves howling in the distance.

The steps made a groan of discomfort as he walked up them, though he was sure that if his coat were any heavier from the rain, the wooden steps would have collapsed under the pressure of his boots. He wasn't sure what he was expecting when he walked inside, maybe a wild animal running around or a frightened parent jumping out at him with a weapon screaming at him to leave, but there was nothing.

He took in his surroundings, and as he did he was sure a wild animal had to have gotten in there from the amount of blood everywhere. It seemed to have covered the walls and floors, he could even see pieces of, what he assumed to be human, flesh and bones. He couldn't smell the blood or rotting flesh, though he wasn't sure if it was just the overpowering smell of rain masking the scent or if it was all just dried up. His eyes scanned around, trying to figure out what had actually happened there. Dishes were shattered, chairs and tables flipped over or broken, even pictures had some form of damage to them as if whatever or whoever attacked this place wanted to make sure every inch of the cottage was damaged.

The crying snapped him out of his thoughts and he began to walk once more while being careful not to disturb anything around him. He made his way through what looked to be the living room, or what was left of it, and walked into a hallway. He stopped once more, the crying was louder now, after taking a small breath he walked down the hallway and stopped at the ajar door. The crying stopped as he lifted his hand and pushed the door open with his finger. The door creaked in disagreement of having to move. It seemed odd to the male, as he stepped into the bedroom, that the room was barely touched, unlike the rest of the cottage.

Lightning flashed outside and the males eyes moved over the room slowly until finally stopping on the source of the crying. The man crouched down slowly but remained silent for a moment as he watched the little movement coming from behind a chest of sorts. Maybe it was a chest of clothing? Or toys? He honestly didn't care about what was in the chest but he was curious to see who it was crying behind the chest. "Don't worry, I won't harm you," he spoke. His voice was rough and stern but also gentle. "Come with me. There's nothing left for you here." He slowly held out a hand.

The man soon discovered it was a small child, perhaps five or six, and it was a boy. The little child seemed unsure at first, maybe feeling safer in the darkness? Or maybe he was just frightened from what had happened in this cottage. The man remained patient and calm as the small boy worked up his courage to step around the chest and walk forward. The man could see the filth that covered the boy, blood and mud, most of his clothing was torn off or ripped bad enough that it was barely staying together, and the man could see some bruises and scratches.

Soon the boy stood in front of him and held up his arms to be lifted. The man arched a brow but then just smiled and wrapped his arms around the boy then wrapped him up in the coat as he was lifted. "You are safe now," he whispered. He turned and began to walk out of the cottage, trying to keep the shivering boy warm against his chest. The crying had stopped, it no longer bothered his ears as he walked away from the cottage and into the woods that surrounded them. The man looked down at the boy who stared up at him with fear but maybe also relief. Such things were unclear to him. He lifted his eyes to look forward as he and the child vanished into the darkness of the night.

CHAPTER ONE

Ten Years Later.

"Your father is going to kill us. Dead. We are so dead and it's all your fault," Liam, glaring at his best friend, said.

"Relax. He won't kill us because he isn't going to find out," Ashton said, laughing.

Ashton was a 5'5" sixteen year old boy with jet black shaggy hair and piercing blue eyes. It was November 2nd and the air was already pretty chilly. It was a quarter to ten at night and already dark outside, but Ashton didn't care about that. He didn't get cold all that quickly so he just wore a plain black shirt, black jeans, and black and orange running shoes. He didn't bother wearing a coat, unlike Liam. Ashton was thin with pale skin and a little muscle but nothing he bragged about.

Liam was an inch taller than Ashton and had just turned sixteen. He was thinner than Ashton with paler skin and pretty much no muscle. He had blonde hair that teased the top of his ears and deep green eyes that needed glasses because, as Ashton liked to say, 'Your eyes are so weak you can't see the light from a flashlight right in front of your face.' They weren't *that* weak. Liam got cold, unlike Ashton, so he wore his blue jeans with a black long sleeve shirt, an ugly yellow sweater that would decorate a garbage can nicely, and a dark blue coat.

"Forgive me for not having the same faith as you, Ashton, but that scary ass giant-of-a-father of yours finds out everything. You remember when we got caught trying to steal his car?"

"How can I forget? You remind me of it every other day. That happened like two years ago. Can't you let it go already? And I wasn't trying to steal it, I was just borrowing it. We only got caught because, one, we tried stealing it out of the driveway, and two, because you suck at being a look out and didn't tell me he was watching us from the door."

"It's not my fault his face screams 'Death to all the maggots that walk this earth.' I swear you should hunt down your real parents. Maybe they're rich! Or maybe they look less scary. Either way it would be a good idea t-"

Ashton blocked him out at this point. Liam always rambled about this when they were doing something that might be considered stupid. Ashton had found out he was adopted five years ago when he had snooped through his father's office and found the paperwork about it. He didn't ask questions about it and he honestly never cared what the reasons were of why he was put up for adoption. As far as he saw it, Stavros was his father and loved him and took great care of him, so why would he complain about that? He was picked to be his son, unlike Liam who was stuck with his abusive drunk father and distant mother who seemed to want nothing to do with Liam anyways.

Liam always rambled about something annoying when they went to do something stupid, this was one of those fun times because they were headed to an old abandoned asylum building. It had been abandoned when Ashton was ten because some of the people who lived there went insane one night and killed over twenty people, some who worked there and some who lived there, and then tried burning the place down. Luckily the cops had already been called and had firefighters and EMTs on standby outside the building so the fire was put out quickly enough. It was supposed to be torn down but someone decided to buy the land. They must have lost funding or something because nothing ever happened with the place and it still stood there with a large fence around it.

"Shh. We're here." Ashton said, cutting Liam off his ramble.

They looked up at the building and on the outside it actually looked normal, mostly. The building was six stories high and made of white brick. The windows all looked like they had been broken and scorch marks from the fire surrounded some of the windows on the third floor, but other than that it looked fine.

"Can't we just go get lucky with some chicks?" Liam whispered. Yeah he didn't like doing all these dumb things that would land him in trouble.

"Chicks?" Ashton smirked. "When have you ever called them 'chicks?' And when have you ever had an interest in them?"

Liam shrugged "I'm allowed to like girls too. Who says I can't like both?"

"I thought being gay kinda meant you didn't like girls?" Ashton asked, raising a brow.

"I'm not gay. I'm bisexual. So I am allowed to like both," Liam muttered.

Ashton chuckled and shook his head "Whatever you say. Anyways, no, we can't leave. We're here now. If you wanted to do something else you should have spoken up sooner."

"I did!"

"Well clearly I wasn't listening." Ashton smirked. "That, or, your idea was stupidly boring. Now stop being a scaredy cat and hurry up before someone sees us." Ashton held back a laugh hearing Liam actually whimper.

He wiggled his way through the broken fence, probably broken because some other kids decided to break in a while ago and cut the fence so they could get in too, and waited for Ashton.

Ashton slipped in behind him and looked around slowly while listening to make sure no one was around them.

"Well we haven't been killed yet so lets go inside" Ashton smiled, heading towards the red front door.

"Inside? You want to go inside? Why? What if other people are in there and they decide to torture us or kills us or even eat us!" Liam's voice was filled with panic and fear, Ashton found it amusing in all honesty.

"I'll just have to outrun you so they'll catch you and I can get away."

"Haha. You are so not funny." Liam rolled his eyes as he spoke.

"I am hilarious." Ashton said with a grin. He nudged Liam and then headed up the stone steps.

Liam looked around as he followed beside Ashton and really hated how Ashton could look so calm and relaxed right now while he was almost trembling in fear. He didn't like going out and trying to see ghosts, since that's why they were even here. People liked to carry on about how they saw ghosts in this building or heard them and so Ashton came up with the brilliant idea to go see if it was true. It was great being his best friend at times, but this wasn't one of those times.

The front door was ajar and was only held up by a large chain that was wrapped around it somehow. Ashton squeezed through the crack first, followed by Liam. They both looked around the area, a long hallway was in front of them with six doors on each side of the walls but most were closed. There was a small lobby and a sitting room, both looked like a tornado had gone through here. Trash, paper, chairs, and old beds were pretty much everywhere. Some blood was on the walls and floors, though most of it looked old, or at least Liam hoped it was old. The only light shining in the place was from a street light but it didn't really show a whole lot around them. They could make out shapes of some things but not much details. Ashton even noticed that some kids had spray painted on the walls and though he couldn't see much of what anything was, he knew the safest guesses were pictures of dicks and boobs everywhere with some writing along the lines of 'Death to those who enter', 'They see you', or 'Suck my dick.'

Ashton already knew anything worth any kind of money would have been looted by now, not that he really cared. He wasn't here to steal stuff, he was here to try seeing if the rumors about ghosts living here was true. So far no luck.

"Okay so we went inside. Can we go now?"

Ashton just ignored Liam and started to walk down the hallway slowly. He sighed when he heard Liam trip over something and curse but didn't bother turning to look.

"I think I hear cops coming. Can we leave? What if they think we are Satan worshipers and shoot us?" Liam whispered.

Ashton rolled his eyes and shook his head slowly "The cops aren't coming and they wouldn't shoot us for worshiping the devil. Stop whining," he murmured. He heard Liam grumbling to himself and chuckled softly. "I find myself with massive headaches every time we hang out."

"And I find a new religion every time we hang out. Why do you think it's a great idea to do these stupid things is beyond me. It's like being convinced that knocking on the devil's door and running away is a great idea."

"I highly doubt the devil lives here and if he does we really should tell him to hire a decorator." Ashton joked.

"Yeah, let's do that, because I'm sure the devil would be so thrilled to stand there and listen to you bitch about how unclean his home is," Liam said sarcastically. He had no idea how he let Ashton convince him to do these things, how could looking for ghosts be fun? Somehow he got convinced to do things that landed them in a ton of trouble whenever they got caught.

Ashton chuckled softly to himself and looked around slowly. He thought about going into some rooms but he really had no need to. Sure it'd be cool to poke around the rooms but he already knew there wasn't anything really worth looking at inside them.

Ashton paused and frowned "Did you hear that?" he whispered.

Liam froze mid step and listened very carefully but after a moment he just glared over at Ashton "Don't play this game with me," he hissed out.

"I'm serious... it sounds like..."

"Two boys in serious trouble?" A deep voice sounded behind them.

CHAPTER TWO

Ashton and Liam stood frozen at the voice. It took them a few minutes before they gathered the courage to slowly turn around and face the man. The man stood 6'9" and had shoulder length black hair. It was too dark to see what the man was wearing but Ashton guessed he was wearing his black dress pants with a long black coat.

"Dad?" Ashton squeaked out.

"So much for him not finding out," Liam whispered under his breath.

"What are you guys doing in here?" Stavros growled out. Oh yeah, he was pissed.

"We... um..." Ashton couldn't think of a lie. Not that lying was even a good idea since his dad always seemed to tell when Ashton lied. "We wanted to check it out."

Stavros crossed his arms over his chest "You wanted to check out the asylum?" He asked. His voice was deep with anger. "You thought it was okay to come look inside? You didn't think that the fence outside was a way to keep people out? Or even the 'keep out' signs that are posted everywhere?"

Ashton opened his mouth to speak but ended up just shutting it. He knew nothing he said right now would make this better.

"Lets go," Stavros growled out. He didn't move as Liam and Ashton slipped past him with their heads down. He remained silent as he followed behind them outside, past the fence, and to his black jag parked on the side of the road. He slipped into the driver's seat while both boys slipped into the back.

Stavros started the car and took off driving. He wasn't going to bring Liam to his father's house, he knew the man was probably drunk right now anyways and he didn't want Liam getting beaten for doing a stupid teenager thing. The boys didn't utter a word as Stavros drove silently towards Liam's mothers. He stopped in front of an ugly soft pink house and felt like cringing. How could anyone have a pink house? Gross. He got out of the car and walked onto the sidewalk, he only stopped to look back to make sure Liam was actually following him, before he pushed the small white gate door open, and waited for Liam to walk ahead of him. He followed two steps behind him and walked inside once Liam had unlocked and opened the front door.

Ashton stayed sitting in the car as he watched Liam and his dad go inside. He felt like shit that Liam was in trouble and he just hoped Dan didn't find out about this. His father was inside for about five minutes before he left the house and returned to the car. He started it up once again and drove home in silence. Ashton thought about what to say but he knew there was nothing he really could say to explain why he did something stupid like this. This wasn't the worst thing he has ever done, so at least that was a plus. Right?

They got home far too quickly for Ashton's liking. His dad pulled into the driveway and shut the car off. They both got out of the car and walked up to the front door. The house had two floors as well as a basement. The outside was always kept clean because his father had hired a groundskeeper. It didn't look like they really needed one because the yard wasn't all that big in the front but the backyard was big enough to have a pond, pool, and a garden. Ashton never bothered to really think about how big the property was but now that he thought about it, it was pretty big and happily they didn't have neighbors right beside them either.

Ashton dreaded going inside because he knew his father was upset with him but he didn't really have a choice except to go inside so he kind of dragged his feet as he walked. He removed his shoes once they got inside and put them away while his dad removed his own shoes and coat.

"Dad... I'm really sorry..." Ashton said softly.

Stavros glared down at him. "Sorry," he repeated. "Ashton..." He sighed and rubbed his temples. "What were you thinking? Why did you think it was a good idea to go there? You know what could have happened right? A lot of homeless people go in there, druggies go in there. What would you have done if they were there? What if the cops showed up?" he said seriously.

Ashton shrugged some. "I wasn't thinking about that..."

"Clearly." Stavros growled out. "You guys could have gotten hurt in there. That isn't a place for you or Liam to be hanging out in and you're lucky I got there before one of you got seriously hurt."

"How did you find us there?" Ashton asked softly. It wasn't like Ashton left a note or anything.

"I activated the gps on your cell." Stavros said. He walked to the left into the living room and sat down on the couch with a sigh. The kitchen was beside the living room and had the back door to it. His dad's office was to the right but the door was always locked and Ashton wasn't allowed in there. His father worked from home. The stairs for upstairs were beside his dad's office with a game room on the other side of the stairs. The door to the basement was in the game room.

"Why?" Ashton asked with a frown.

Stavros rose a brow as he looked at him. "Why?" he repeated and shook his head. "I had it activated after you and Liam decided to stay out all night without saying anything to me about it." That hadn't been a good time. Ashton and Liam had decided to get drunk and ended up hanging around the creek all night. It was a fun night but it was not fun once he got home. He had never seen his father get that angry before and he never wanted to see that again.

"Are you trying to worry me to death about you?" Stavros asked. "Because you are doing a great job at it. I know, you are a teenager, but damn it Ashton you don't need to be causing some kind of trouble every other week. There is plenty for you and Liam to do that doesn't involve pissing me off or getting yourselves killed."

Ashton heard this so many times. He knew his dad was right but he thought by now his father would have a different lecture to give or something. He heard his father speaking again and made the mistake of not really paying attention because his father just stared at him.

"What?" Ashton asked.

"Well?" Stavros growled out.

Ashton shrugged slightly "I... Don't know what you asked," he admitted.

Stavros stood quickly. "Go to your room. Right now!" He snapped out.

Ashton quickly obeyed and ran upstairs to avoid angering his dad even more.

Stavros ran his fingers through his hair and growled under his breath. He ended up sighing when his cell rang and quickly answered it. He didn't speak at first, just listened to the voice on the other end before he laughed darkly.

"Are you serious?" Stavros growled. He narrowed his eyes as he listened. He walked over to his office and stepped inside once he unlocked it. His office was full of shelves that had a lot of books on it, some looked really old and worn out while others looked like they hadn't been touched. He had a large brown desk with a laptop on it, some papers, and pens. He didn't bother turning on the ceiling light, he just turned the small desk light on and sat down on the desk chair.

He rubbed his face as he sighed again. "I really don't have time for this right now. Stop by tomorrow at noon." He hung up before the person could respond. He groaned as he sat back in his chair and shut his eyes to think.

Ashton had changed into some pj bottoms and was sitting on his bed. His room was covered in band posters, it had a small simple desk in the corner for his laptop and for him to do his homework and a dresser beside it. The door to his closet was at the end of his bed.

He had been texting Liam for a few minutes but he assumed Liam's mom took his cell away because Liam stopped talking. Ashton had no idea how long it would be before his dad took away his cell. It was 11:30pm now and he knew he should be sleeping but he couldn't sleep. He finally heard his dad heading upstairs and thought he'd come in his room but his dad just walked past his door and went to his own room. Great, now he had to wait until tomorrow to finish talking about this.

Ashton sighed. "Oh you can be so stupid at times," he muttered to himself. He put his cell on the nightstand and then laid down under the blanket to try and get some sleep.

CHAPTER THREE

Ashton poked at his eggs as he sat at the table and sighed. He wasn't hungry but he knew he had to eat something. It had been a week since him and Liam got caught breaking into the asylum. His father had grounded him for two weeks without his phone or laptop though Ashton wasn't going to complain about it. He still went to school and used his laptop in the living room while doing homework but that was it. This was his boring life for one more week. He knew Liam was grounded too and was still at his moms house. She wasn't happy at all either but at least she wasn't willing to tell Liam's father about what happened. Ashton forced himself to eat some of his breakfast but ended up throwing the rest out and washed the dishes. He heard his dad talking to people in his office, which seemed to be happening every day this week, though he had no idea who was in there. Ashton always went to school before he saw who his dad was talking to but it was Saturday now so maybe he'd see who it was this time. Not that he fully cared.

He was just about to head upstairs when he heard his dad's office door open. He blinked and stood by the stairs as he watched two men walk out of the room followed by his father. They both stood at 6'7" but one had short brown hair and the other had short black hair.

The guy with brown hair had tanned skin and sharp facial features with about two days worth of beard growing on his face. He wore a brown shirt with blue jeans and looked to be twenty five with brown eyes.

The other guy was wearing a white shirt with black pants and wasn't as tanned as the other and had a black goatee with hazel eyes and had a slightly longer face than the other guy but they both looked really similar to each other so, Ashton assumed they might be brothers, he also looked to be twenty five.

Ashton didn't stay downstairs long enough to talk though. He quickly went upstairs to his room and listened to the two men leave. He heard his father moving around downstairs so he decided to go back downstairs with his homework and sat in the living room.

"Who were those guys?" Ashton asked.

Stavros poured himself a cup of coffee as he spoke. "Just a few guys I use to work with. They travel a lot for work and decided to stop by here to say hi."

Ashton opened his books to start working on his homework and sighed softly. "I'm almost done my homework..." He said. He didn't care enough about the two guys to ask more questions about them.

"Good. When that is done go back to your room," Stavros said. He headed to his office and paused at the door to look at Ashton. "Tyler and Patrick will be coming over for dinner tonight." With that he went into his office and shut the door.

Ashton grumbled but said nothing. He didn't want people over but it's not like he could tell his dad no.

Ashton finished up his homework and returned to his room where he pretty much just read and fell asleep. He skipped lunch because he honestly wasn't hungry but he did go down to get a glass of juice and noticed his father was still in his office. He remembered when he was younger he used to spend hours imagining what his father did in there. He came up with crazy ideas like his dad battled dragons in there or had a door to another world and so on but now that he was older he knew that wasn't true at all. He did boring work all day long. Ashton finished up his juice and went back up to his room.

"Ashton come down for dinner!" Stavros called from the bottom of the stairs.

Ashton jumped awake and blinked as he took a minute to register what was going on. He didn't even remember falling asleep again. Great, now he wasn't going to sleep at all at bedtime. Ashton sighed and pulled on a clean shirt and headed downstairs. He frowned some seeing those two men sitting at the table and sighed. How did he forget his father invited them? He sat down in his normal spot and glanced at the two men.

"Ashton, this is Patrick and Tyler. Guys, this is my son Ashton," Stavros said, pointing at each guy as he said their names. Patrick was the one with black hair and Tyler was the brown haired guy.

"Nice meeting you, Ashton," Tyler said. His voice was deep and had some kind of accent that Ashton had never heard before. Then again he was only sixteen and hadn't traveled around much so he wasn't too surprised he couldn't place the accent.

"Hi," Patrick murmured, with the same accent as Tyler.

Ashton just smiled and looked down at his plate. His dad had made roast with mashed potatoes, caesar salad, and gravy.

Ashton waited for his father to be seated before he started eating. He had nothing to say to the two guys so he just remained silent.

"So how is work going?" Stavros asked, pouring himself some coffee.

Tyler shrugged. "It's slow right now but we've found a few promising projects to take up."

"Oh? Here?"

"Yes." Patrick murmured. He didn't seem to really like talking.

Ashton tilted his head a little as he watched Patrick struggle with eating. It was… interesting. The guy didn't seem to know how to properly hold a fork but Ashton wasn't about to be a dick and make fun of the guy.

Tyler helped Patrick out. "We just have to wait for the paperwork and permission for it," Tyler explained.

Stavros rose a brow and spoke once he finished his mouthful. "That's why you're here." It wasn't a question. "Well I'm sure you'll get an answer soon."

Tyler smirked lightly. "We're hoping so. We'd like to stay here for a while."

Stavros nodded but focused on eating for now.

It was really awkward, they all just sat there and ate…. With very little talking… Ashton was more than happy when he finally finished eating and excused himself.

"Oh Ashton, before you leave." Stavros smiled. "Tyler and I are going to be away for business for three days. I know you just met Patrick but he is a dear friend of mine and he will be staying here to watch you while I'm gone so behave for him. Okay?"

Ashton was happy, for a minute, because he assumed his father leaving would mean he could stay at Liam's, but that hope was quickly destroyed when his father said Patrick was watching him instead. He had never heard of the guy before but now he was supposed to be okay with being watched by the guy? Ashton just nodded and quickly went up to his room.

Patrick grumbled. "Do I have to stay here?"

"Yes" Stavros and Tyler said at once.

Patrick grumbled again.

"Relax. Ashton is a good kid. It'll be fine. He's grounded right now so he isn't allowed out of his room except for school and meals."

"You want me to watch an annoying teenager thing when I can't even kick him out of the house? Why are you torturing me like this!" Patrick groaned.

Tyler laughed. "Calm down Patrick. If he is grounded it means he'll stay in his room all day and you can ignore him or pretend he doesn't exist."

Stavros rolled his eyes as he started putting things away with Tyler's help. "You do have to feed him…"

"I can't cook!" Patrick hissed.

Tyler laughed again. "Yeah, you really don't want him to try cooking."

"How did you manage to live all these years without cooking anything?"

"I live with Tyler… He cooks." Patrick shrugged.

Stavros sighed. "Well luckily for you the leftovers from tonight's meal will last for a day or two and if it doesn't I have fixings for sandwiches in the fridge so use that."

Tyler smirked. "You really trust him alone with your son?"

"No. Not at all. However this is a favor for you two that I am doing and I can't bring Ashton with us nor can I leave him home alone because he might actually burn down the house so one of you two are going to stay here with him," Stavros responded.

Tyler and Patrick looked at each other, then looked back at Stavros.

"And you thought the best choice was Patrick?"

"Why does it have to be me?"

Both questions came at once. Stavros rubbed his temples and sighed. "Patrick has always done better with children."

"He doesn't even like children!" Tyler laughed out.

Stavros glared at him. "At least he won't order strippers to keep the kid busy while you go out!"

"That happened once! One time!" Tyler huffed.

"The child was six!"

"Hey he was smiling the whole time!" Tyler narrowed his eyes as he spoke.

"It was a girl." Stavros sighed heavily. He was getting a headache. The strippers ended up leaving when they realized Tyler left them but they weren't happy.

"Patrick may lack the skills of cooking but at least he pretends to be friendly..." Stavros said. He walked to the living room and sat down.

Patrick blinked. "I pretend to be friendly?" He smiled.

Tyler frowned. "He taught an eleven year old every swear word he could think of two days ago and he keeps handing out scissors and telling the kids to run as fast as they can."

Stavros groaned. "Seriously, Patrick?" He sighed. How can two grown men act like young teenagers? "Maybe I'll just stay home and you guys can go..." He muttered.

"You know we can't go unless we have you or Killian and he isn't around here right now so that just leaves you. Patrick can stay with

Ashton and take care of him, hopefully without killing him, and you and I will go." Tyler replied. He sat down on the chair and glared at Patrick. "Don't kill him."

"You guys take all my fun away." Patrick sighed out. "I guess we're staying here for the night?" He asked.

Tyler nodded. "If Stavros is okay with it, yes."

"That's fine. I don't have a spare room but I can set up the game room for the night for you two," Stavros offered.

The two nodded.

They talked for another hour or so before Stavros got them set up with some blankets and pillows in the game room. It had a pull out couch in it, though neither one seemed thrilled about having to share a bed.

Stavros bid them goodnight and headed up to his own room to sleep. He wouldn't deny he was nervous about leaving Ashton alone with Patrick and they did act like idiots a lot of the time but he knew Patrick would take good care of Ashton for a few days.

CHAPTER FOUR

Ashton was awoken at five in the morning by his father, who was just waking him to inform him that he and Tyler were leaving now and reminded him to behave and listen to Patrick. Ashton ended up going right back to bed after giving his dad a hug and telling him to be careful.

Ashton had no idea how long he slept for but he woke up smelling something burning and hearing Patrick cursing as the fire alarm went off. He groaned as he rolled out of bed and made a face as he headed downstairs and saw the house was filled with black smoke and the smell... He had no idea what it even was from.

"What are you doing?" Ashton coughed out. He opened the back door quickly and grabbed a dish cloth to wave the smoke away from the fire alarm.

"I was making breakfast," Patrick said. He smiled. "I think it's ready now." He sounded way too happy about this.

Ashton took a moment to get over being stunned. "I think it was ready ten minutes ago. What are you even making?"

"I was heating up some of the supper from last night." Patrick shrugged. "Tyler told me to just use the microwave." He added.

Ashton walked over to it and blinked. "How long did you put it in for?"

"Oh I don't know. I pushed a few buttons and sat down to watch tv and then suddenly smoke starts going everywhere..."

"What buttons did you push?" Ashton asked.

"Um… I think the five, three, maybe the eight and six?" Patrick shrugged again. "Is it supposed to be this black? It didn't look like this last night…"

"How… what?" Ashton tried wrapping his mind around this. His father left this guy here to watch him? Really? The guy couldn't even use the microwave properly!

"No it's not supposed to be this black… You're only supposed to put it in for a minute or two." Ashton explained. Happily the smoke was slowly clearing out and the stupid alarm stopped blaring. "Have you never used a microwave before?"

"No," Patrick sighed. "Tyler tried teaching me this shit but it's all too complicated." He sighed again.

Ashton grumbled and carefully used the dish cloth to get the plate out of the microwave and set it aside so it could cool down before he threw it out.

Ashton muttered under his breath as he got another plate out and put some food on it. "Okay so when you use the microwave to heat something up just put one minute to start. Okay? If it's still cold than add another minute to it." He explained.

Patrick tilted his head as he watched Ashton heat up the food. He made it seem so easy but the boy probably used this often so of course he'd know how it worked.

Ashton finished heating up the plates of food and sat at the table across from Patrick. It was weird being here without his dad and he was a bit upset that his father didn't trust him enough to leave him alone for a few days but Ashton knew it was because he caused enough trouble as it was even when his father was around.

"So how old are you?" Ashton asked.

"Twenty five. How old are you?" Patrick asked. He used his hands this time to eat his food. It was… Odd.

"I'm sixteen.." Ashton said. "How are you that old and don't know how to use a microwave?" He asked curiously.

"*That* old? I am not old!" Patrick muttered. If only Ashton knew. "I moved around with Tyler a lot. He always did the cooking." Patrick explained.

"He never taught you to use silverware?" Ashton asked. He hadn't met any grown ups who used their hands to eat roast.

Patrick grinned and looked up from his plate. "Yes, he tried teaching me, but I guess I'm too stubborn because I never caught on to it."

Ashton just nodded and went back to eating in silence. He really hoped the place didn't get burned down while his father was away.

"So, Stavros told me you are grounded?" Patrick asked. He smirked. "What did you do?"

"I broke into the old asylum," Ashton said with a slight shrug.

Patrick choked on his food as he burst out laughing.

"It isn't funny," Ashton muttered.

Patrick shook his head. "I highly disagree." He laughed out. "That is fucking awesome."

Ashton smiled slightly and shrugged again. "My dad didn't think so."

"Yeah well he has a stick up his ass."

It was Ashton's turn to choke on his food. "What?" He coughed out. He quickly took a sip of his water.

Patrick shrugged. "It's true. Teenagers always do stupid stuff and teenage boys seem to do really stupid stuff as often as possible. It shouldn't be surprising to him that you would do something that stupid." Patrick chuckled. "So what was it like?"

"It was dark… Kinda creepy." Ashton shrugged. "We didn't really get far because my dad showed up shortly after we got in."

"We?" Patrick asked.

"My best friend, Liam, and myself." Ashton responded.

"Liam? Liam Tase?" Patrick asked.

"You know him?"

"Yes. Tyler is making arrangements to get Dan into rehab for his drinking. Liam is going to be staying with me while that happens because his mother didn't seem thrilled on the idea of Liam staying with her." Patrick explained. He had already met the family a few days ago. Liam seemed shy and quiet at first and his mother seemed a little too thrilled about being rid of Liam while Dan was in rehab. Patrick didn't understand the family whatsoever but Liam had agreed to it all.

"His dad agreed to go to rehab? Really? Liam's been trying to make that happen for a few years now," Ashton said. It was a little confusing but it also made Ashton sad that his mother didn't want Liam around. He never understood how people like Liam's parents could ever have children.

"He refused at first." Patrick said. "It took a lot of convincing on Tyler's part but since Tyler promised he was paying for all of it, Dan agreed. It's where Tyler and Stavros went. The rehab is four hours away from here and for the first few days they have to stay there to make sure everything goes smoothly," Patrick explained.

"Where is Liam now than? Since you're here with me." Ashton asked.

"He is at home packing a few things and staying with his mother until I leave here. I'm taking him back to my place. He'll take a few days to settle and get use to everything going on so he'll be out of school for the week."

Ashton remained silent for a few minutes. He was happy that Dan was getting help but at the same time he was bummed out that he wouldn't see Liam in school for a week. How was he supposed to get by in school if he couldn't hang out with his best friend? Sure he had other friends but still…

Ashton cleaned up the dishes once they finished eating and sighed. "Well I'm going back to my room now… I guess," he murmured.

Patrick nodded. "I'd let you hang out down here but if your dad ever found out he may just beat my ass for it so… Have fun being bored in your room."

Ashton grumbled and walked up a few steps before pausing and looking at Patrick as he headed towards the living room. "If you need help cooking anything… Just ask okay? If you have no idea how to use it don't just try using it." With that he headed to his room.

Patrick grumbled as he flipped through the channels on the TV, but it was beyond boring. How did people do nothing but watch TV all day? He didn't get it. "Well might as well take a nap," he muttered. He was supposed to stay inside all day and do nothing? This was the worst kind of punishment ever. He'd rather take an ass whipping any day instead of being grounded for two weeks. Instead of just sitting there he decided to get up and just explore the house. Nothing was all that interesting inside the house but he knew even if he tried laying down to nap he'd get so bored of it and end up staring at the wall the whole time. "I hate you, Stavros" he murmured to himself. "Next time just spank the kid and be done with it." he sighed. This was why he didn't have children. Well okay, so he had many reasons why he didn't have children, one is because he hated kids. He knew how to sort of act around them but those tiny little annoying things were boring.

"At times like this, I wished my house was haunted." Ashton murmured, laying on his bed. "At least a ghost would keep me some kind of company while I sat here doing nothing..." He sighed. He tossed and turned on his bed but he couldn't relax enough to sleep. This was going to be a very long three days, it was going to be even longer at school without Liam.

CHAPTER FIVE

Ashton had no idea how much more he could take of Patrick. His father and Tyler were suppose to show up at some point today and Ashton really hoped that happened soon because he was sure he was close to killing Patrick. Ashton ended up making all their meals because Patrick tried to heat up a sandwich, Ashton had no idea why he tried doing it and when he asked all Patrick said was 'I'm making a hot sandwich'. Ashton was sure this guy would be dead if his brother didn't stay with him and cooked all their food. Ashton also discovered that Patrick liked doing a lot of weird things, like blaring weird music and sing as loud as he could, or yell at random things if they 'disobeyed' him. Patrick also liked to sleep naked, which scared the crap out of Ashton when he woke up at night to go to the bathroom only to find Patrick already in there using it.. With the door wide open… naked. Ashton would have that image buned into his brain for the rest of his life.

At the current moment Ashton was trying really hard not to fall asleep in his last class. It was English and he had been going to this school for two years now and had this teacher last year as well and she still mispronounce his name. She always said 'Jas-per' instead of 'Jas-fur' but he gave up on correcting her. Instead he decided to say her name wrong every time she said his wrong. She didn't seem happy about it but he didn't care, he figured after two years of him being in her class she would at least learn how to say it right.

Ashton watched the clock on the wall, only ten minutes left of class. Great.. He wasn't really in a rush to get home. He was half afraid the place would be burnt down by now but he had made sure to leave some food in the fridge for Patrick, stuff he wouldn't need to actually heat up.

"Please be home.." he whispered to himself. He wasn't sure he could last another hour alone with crazy Patrick and he really was judging his father's choice of friends.

Ashton sighed hearing the bell ring and gathered up his books before he left the room. He stopped at his locker for a minute to grab his bag and then started walking home. He only lived a few blocks away from his school so walking wasn't all that bad.

"Oh surprise, surprise. It's not burnt down." Ashton said as he approached his house. He groaned hearing the loud music playing. He had no idea what Patrick was listening to but it sounded like a dying cat singing and it wasn't pleasant. He walked inside, letting out a breath of relief seeing Patrick actually wearing clothes, and pulled off his shoes before he headed straight up to his room. Patrick had yelled something to him but he didn't bother checking what it was. He had only been around Patrick for three days but he discovered that Patrick yelled about random things all the time or just started weird conversations. He was greatly disturbed about all the 'fun' things he liked to teach kids but he couldn't deny that he did actually like him a little.. Even if he was crazy.

Ashton stayed in his room and worked on his homework at his desk. He rolled his eyes when he heard Patrick yelling at something again, he really should write all this stuff down because at times it was very amusing listening to it but right now he had to focus on his homework and get that done.

It was a few hours later when he finally heard the music turn off and realized he heard people talking downstairs. He smiled as he quickly left his room and went downstairs and saw his father with Tyler in the living room.

"At least he didn't burn down your house." Tyler chuckled.

"Yeah, that's great, instead he decided to move all the furniture out of the living room to dance?" Stavros sighed. He was tired, the trip had been long and tiring and now he had to fix his living room.

"He almost burned down the house." Ashton said, stepping into the living room.

"Of course he did" Tyler sighed. "Well let's leave Patrick, before Stavros decides to rip your arms off." he chuckled.

"At least Ashton is still alive.." Patrick pointed out. "He didn't starve or anything." He smiled. Ashton wasn't sure why he was so proud of that, Ashton didn't starve to death because he cooked his own meals.

"That's a plus." Stavros grumbled. He walked them to the front door and opened it "Well thank you Patrick, for keeping my son alive." he said.

Patrick shrugged and walked out of the house.

"Bye" Ashton called after him. He finally could relax and not have to worry about things burning or walking into the bathroom to see a naked man standing there. Ashton shuddered at the memory. Oh yeah, he was scarred for life.

"See yeah" Tyler called over his shoulder and walked out.

Stavros shut the door and groaned as he looked back at the living room. He really just wanted to sleep but first he had to put his living room back together. "So how was your weekend?" Stavros asked. He walked into the living room and started pushing the furniture back into their normal spots with Ashton's help.

"It was fine." Ashton said. He decided not to give all the details about his weekend with Patrick, but he did go over some things.

"That's good." Stavros said, once Ashton stopped speaking. "I'm exhausted so we'll have an early supper today and then I'll probably go to bed. You got all your homework done?"

Ashton nodded. "Hey dad? Why didn't you tell me that Dan was going into rehab?"

Stavros sighed "Oh that man can't keep his damn mouth shut." he grumbled. "I didn't tell you because Liam wanted to make sure it would actually work before going around and telling everyone. I only found out because Tyler suggested I help out with it and Liam agreed."

"Why not offer to let Liam stay with us?"

"I did but Patrick thought it'd be a better idea to keep Liam at his place for now. Patrick can bring Liam to the rehab center a lot more often than I can and he can also take better care of him and help him a lot better than I can. Liam needs help adjusting to the new changes and also needs help coping with all of this. Patrick has that training, I don't. Plus, Liam seems a little afraid of me most times." Stavros explained. "I know Patrick can be a little…"

"Crazy?"

"Yes, but he can help Liam and focus all his attention on Liam. If Liam came here I'd have to split my focus between the two of you and right now Liam needs full time care."

Ashton nodded as he listened. He understood that but he wasn't happy about it. He only spent a few days with Patrick and already felt crazy from it. "Patrick doesn't even know how to cook…" Ashton pointed out.

Stavros laughed softly "He knows how to cook. He just really hates cooking. He rather starve instead of actually cooking food. He also really hates the quiet which is why he blares music so loud."

"Oh. I'm so glad you decided to tell me this *before* leaving me alone with him."

"I didn't find out until after we left actually. I wasn't worried though, you know how to cook and look! You're still alive!" Stavros smiled.

Ashton looked bemused, "Now I wish he burned down the house."

Stavros laughed "Alright enough chit chat. Let's just make something quick and get to bed before I just collapse where I'm standing."

Ashton wouldn't argue about that. He just wanted to sleep the rest of the week away so he could be ungrounded and actually see Liam.

"You really think the rehab will work?" Ashton asked, as he helped make sandwiches.

Stavros frowned and remained silent for a few minutes while he thought about it. He knew it could work if Dan actually gave it a shot but at this point there was no telling what that man would do. "It could as long as Dan actually tries. If he doesn't bother giving it a full effort it wont work so then we'd go to plan B"

"What's plan B?" Ashton asked.

Stavros carried his sandwich to the table and sat down "Plan B is just leaving Dan alone. If he wants to suffer being a drunk and not want help we can't force him. If that happens then Tyler and I will go to the police and have Liam removed from that home. It's something that should have happened a long time ago but Liam has always been unwilling to actually admit his life at home to anyone but now he is willing to talk about it with Patrick. If Liam's mother is unwilling to take him in then either Tyler or myself will do whatever we can to get him so at least he is staying with someone he knows. It is something we've already talked about with both Liam and Dan. If Liam comes stays here with us we'd have to change the game room into an actual bedroom for him. I know how hard it would be for you and Liam if he stayed with Tyler and Patrick simply because they travel for work.. Which means if they take Liam in, they wouldn't stay here… they'd go back home in New York." he explained softly.

Ashton really wished that was something that wouldn't happen. He was not ready to be living fifteen hours away from his best friend. He knew as life went on his friends would change but he pretty much grew up with Liam. They were basically brothers and he wasn't ready to let that go and he hoped Liam wasn't either. "I hope that doesn't happen." He finally whispered. It hurt to even think about Liam leaving.

Stavros nodded "It's why we are trying really hard to make things work out." Stavros replied. He knew how hurt his son was just thinking about never seeing Liam again so he really was going to work hard on making sure that didn't happen.

They ate the rest of their food in silence, Ashton was deep in thought and Stavros was just way too tired to think about anything right now. He made sure the house was locked up and turned off all the lights as they headed upstairs. Stavros took a quick shower and then headed to his room to sleep.

Ashton went to his own room and just stared at the wall as he thought over what his father had said. He really didn't like Dan but he never talked to Liam about that stuff. He tried to, a few times in the past, convince Liam to go to the police or move away from his father but Liam had always refused. Ashton didn't understand why but last time he questioned Liam about it they ended up getting into a huge fight and didn't talk for over a month so Ashton decided he'd lend his support and help out Liam as much as he could without talking about that stuff. He remembered when Liam first showed up to his house with a bruised eye and busted lip, Stavros lost his shit seeing it and Liam had to actually beg Stavros not to do anything about it. Stavros didn't listen, of course, but when he brought Liam to the police station Liam just lied about what was going on. He really hated to talk about his home life and since than Stavros didn't get involved unless Liam actually asked for help. No one could force Liam to admit anything, they couldn't force him to talk to the cops or move away so they just did what they could and made sure Liam knew they were there to help whenever he needed them.

Ashton groaned as his thoughts screamed in his mind and pulled his pillow over his head "Go to sleep" he groaned at himself. He tossed and turned for a few hours before he finally actually fell asleep.

"Where am I? What's happening?" everything was pitch black. He had to strain his eyes to see anything in the dark room. He heard screaming, a woman screaming, but he didn't know who it was. Where was he again? He jumped hearing the loud crack of thunder and hit a trunk in front of him. He frowned as he slowly stood up and waited until lightning flashed before he looked around. Everything seemed perfectly find in the room, nothing tossed over or destroyed but he could hear things being thrown around, heard voices yelling and more screaming. He felt his heart pounding in his chest as he slowly stepped forward towards the door. He realized he was in a bedroom when he ended up stumbling back onto the bed hearing some horrible cry, he assumed the woman made the sound. He gasped for breath, now realizing he was holding it in. Everything was still so black but his hearing now focused on the rain pouring down against the house as it fell silent. He heard heavy footsteps, his breathing quickened as he realized they were approaching the room. What was going on? He knew this place but he couldn't remember how he knew it. His breath caught in his throat when

he heard the door opening, his eyes wide with fear as he tried making out what was going on. He saw a dark shadow of a man as the door opened and then suddenly the man was rushing towards him "NO!" he screamed.

Ashton jumped awake, panting, as the nightmare flew through his mind. He didn't understand anything about the dream he had. He knew that place… somehow but he honestly couldn't remember how he knew it. He remembered the screams, remembered the room… it all seemed so familiar and yet he couldn't place any of it. His heart pounded in his ears as he looked around his room, it took a few minutes for him to calm down, but he realized where he was and slowly calmed down. "Just a dream" he whispered to himself. He rubbed his face before he laid down and stared at the wall again "Just a dream." he repeated. He shut his eyes to try and sleep again but he already knew he wasn't getting anymore sleep. It may have just been a dream but it had felt so real to him for some reason.

CHAPTER SIX

It was finally here! The last day of his grounding! Who knew two weeks could drag on so slowly? He hadn't seen Liam at all during the week and his father had promised that if Ashton behaved he'd be allowed out today to go see Liam. Ashton had made sure he behaved. He completely forgotten about the nightmare he had at the start of the week and normally he'd tell his father about it because this wasn't the first time he has had this type of nightmare but his father never seemed to say much about it so he decided from now on he just wouldn't bother telling him anymore. It was just a silly nightmare anyways, they'd go away.. Right?.

Ashton was sitting in the game room playing on his gamecube as he waited for Patrick to bring Liam over. Patrick lived just outside town, apparently Tyler and Patrick rented houses while they traveled and they liked being outside of towns so Ashton couldn't just walk to see Liam. He was half curious about what they did for a living but his father never answered that question. He just always said something about how they just have to travel for work so Ashton had fun just coming up with random ideas of what they did. So far his favorite was that they sold sex toys to the sex shops. He knew it most likely wasn't true but until he learned what they actually did, that's what he was sticking with.

Ashton smiled wide hearing a knock on the front door and quickly paused his game as he jumped up and ran to the front door. He skipped to a stop and swung it open "Liam!" Ashton smiled wide.

Liam looked pretty good so far. His hair was longer, which looked a little weird, but he actually looked more relaxed and happy which was great. Liam chuckled and hugged Ashton tightly "Is it weird we react this way to seeing each other after two weeks?" Liam asked with a chuckle.

Ashton shrugged as he pulled away from the hug "Probably but I won't complain if you don't." He stepped aside for them to walk into the house and then closed the door behind them.

They removed their shoes and Patrick went to the living room as Stavros walked downstairs. Ashton and Liam retreated to the game room.

"So how are things going?" Ashton asked. "You look okay. Patrick is feeding you and everything?"

Liam laughed, "No, Patrick doesn't cook. I mean he can… if he actually tries to but it's pretty much me that cooks everything other than when Tyler is around but he spends a lot of time helping my dad."

"Patrick hasn't driven you crazy?"

"Oh yeah he has. I don't know what music he listens to but it's horrible and I discovered that he really hates clothes. Tyler yelled at him a few times because Patrick magically "forgot" he wasn't alone at the house and decided to walk around naked. I know I'm quiet but damn I didn't realize it was so easy to forget I was around." Liam laughed. "Other than that, and his annoying habit of always yelling at everything, everything is fine. I get to see my dad in a few days so I'm excited about that… Tyler told me he was doing really well so far."

"That's good. I was a little worried about that." Ashton admitted. "Hopefully soon he can come home," he said with a smile.

Liam nodded, "I'm hoping so. I'm grateful that Patrick and Tyler have been really helpful but I do miss being at home in my own bed. Tyler is a huge clean freak and freaks out anytime we leave even one dirty dish at the sink. Patrick seems to like to dirty everything before Tyler returns home and then I get to listen to Tyler and Patrick yell at each other for an hour before Tyler comes scold me for not keeping things clean." Liam sighed.

Ashton laughed softly, "It's a good thing he's never been in your room than because you hardly keep that clean." He joked.

Liam playfully shoved him "It's not like your room is spotless either!" he laughed out.

Ashton shrugged. It was true so he wasn't even about to argue that.

"How is Liam doing?" Stavros asked. He sat on his couch with a glass of water while Patrick sat on the chair and sipped a glass of juice.

"He is doing alright. He has some down moments but he is really trying hard to work through everything. He finally opened up and told me all about his life and I think that helped. He doesn't carry that stress with him anymore so he is a lot more relaxed about everything and he doesn't get all jumpy when Tyler and I yell around him." Patrick replied. "He gets some nightmares about it all but even those are starting to go away."

Stavros nodded, "That's good. A boy his age shouldn't be worrying about all this stuff. Have you talked to his mother at all?"

Patrick shook his head slowly, "I tried a few times but she only answered the phone once and that was to tell me to stop calling her. She really seems to want nothing to do with Liam or his father. I don't know the whole family story but it has to be interesting for it to be this way.. Right?." Patrick shrugged. "Surely she can't be this heartless towards her son."

Stavros sighed and shook his head, "All I know is that his father has always been a drunk and his mother left them both as fast as she could. She'll tolerate Liam for a short time but for whatever reason she seems to really dislike him. Which is sad because Liam is a great kid and deserves to be loved, not shunned by his own mother." Stavros growled some. He'd never understand that woman nor did he really care to.

"Hey I heard there was a murder a few days ago?" Patrick asked.

Stavros nodded "I haven't mentioned it to Ashton, but yes, a few days ago a man was killed. It wasn't just the one murder though, there have been three before that and two since. So far everyone seems to think they are random killings and don't have enough information to put it on the news just yet." Stavros said. "Do you know anything about them?"

"Me? Why would I? I've been out taking care of Liam and Tyler has been gone to check on Dan every few days." Patrick replied. "Have you asked Killian?"

"He hasn't been around here for over a year, I highly doubt he knows a thing about it." Stavros said with a sigh. He relaxed back against the couch and rubbed his face "I'll have to mention it to Ashton though. He's off grounding now and I don't need him thinking it's okay to be walking the streets after dark. Especially since the police don't even have suspects."

"I guess I'll have to mention it to Liam as well." Patrick grumbled. Did every parent tell kids about these things? It didn't seem like a great idea but then again Liam and Ashton did seem to like to stay out late..

"You'd think there'd be some kind of warning in school about them…" Patrick muttered.

Stavros rose a brow, "No. It's up to the parents to decide if they want to tell their children or not. Not all parents would be thrilled if the school just decided to mention the killings going on to their kids. It can cause panic and fear and cause a lot of kids to refuse to leave their rooms." he pointed out.

"Yeah, yeah, Whatever." Patrick grumbled, waving his hand in dismissal. He didn't have kids so what did he know about it?

Stavros just rolled his eyes.

The two talked for a few more hours, deciding to leave the teens alone for now, before they got up and worked on making supper for them all. Patrick didn't really help all that much, he just decided to keep bothering Stavros about how he was cooking things wrong. Stavros ignored him simply because he knew Patrick just wanted to get under his skin about everything right now.

Ashton and Liam finally came into the kitchen a few minutes before supper was ready to set the table, since Patrick clearly wasn't doing it.

Stavros made some homemade stew and finally made Patrick do something, butter bread, that wasn't too hard for him.

Once it was all ready, they all sat down and ate. Ashton and Liam talked about how they almost died while being grounded, because it was the worst thing in the world. Stavros and Patrick remained silent for the most part and once they finished eating, put things away, and cleaned up the kitchen, Stavros had the boys go into the living room and talked with them about the murders going around.

Ashton was the first to speak, after having sat there for a few minutes to digest what he just heard, "Murders? What? Why?"

"It seems some people got tired of other people living." Patrick said.

Stavros glared at Patrick but spoke to Ashton, "We don't know much because the cops don't know much. We just know some people have been killed."

"Do they know who?" Liam asked. He was silently reminding himself never to go out alone anywhere.

Stavros shook his head, "They haven't said." he replied.

Ashton had no idea how he was supposed to feel about this. Sure, he knew murders happened a lot around the world but it just seemed so odd that it'd happen here like this.

"Is it like… " Liam trailed off. What was he supposed to call this? It just seemed to happen too often for it to be random killings.

"I know you boys are afraid." Stavros spoke softly. "You have a right to be afraid. I know there has been talk about the school closing until this is all settled if it keeps on like this. You two must understand now that it's extremely important to not go running off and sneaking into abandoned buildings or causing other kinds of trouble. We don't know what the killer is after, what he/she looks like, we know nothing so stay close to home."

Ashton gave a nod but he remained silent. What if someone broke into their house to kill them? Or killed during the day? Or… Ashton had to clear his head because he knew he'd get himself all panicked if he kept on with these questions. He couldn't change any of this and had no control over it but he could at least try keeping himself safe and staying close to home.

Liam also remained silent as he went over Stavros' words. Murders did happen, they all knew that, but this many murders in such a short time? Here? It seemed odd. Someone was differently after revenge or something. Liam had caught him briefly wishing his mother went out late at night. Liam was shocked about that thought and wondered if he truly wished that. Sure she wasn't a nice woman but did he actually want her to die? Liam looked up, his eyes locking with Patrick's for a moment and when Liam looked away he had seen a small grin on Patrick's face, as if the man had actually heard Liam's thought.

Stavros was surprised that the boys handled the news rather well. They asked a few small questions but in the end they just went back to the game room to hang out. Patrick pulled on his black boots and said bye to everyone before leaving, Liam was staying there for a few days while Patrick went with Tyler to check on Dan again. Stavros didn't mind it at all.

Stavros walked to his office and decided to do some work since the boys were playing their weird video games.

"Who do you think is doing it?" Liam asked.

Ashton shrugged, "I honestly have no guesses. I mean it wouldn't fully surprise me if it turns out to be one of those asshole bullies at our school doing it but I didn't even know about them until now so... no clue."

Liam frowned some, he wouldn't have been surprised either, but he said nothing more about that. He really didn't want to focus on that stuff right now. It wasn't long before they got bored of the games and knew bedtime was approaching so they got the pull out bed all set up for Liam and went to bed.

Liam woke up the next morning hearing someone walking around the kitchen. He planned on staying in bed to get some more sleep but once the smell of breakfast hit his nose, he was up and changed into clean clothes. He walked out of the room and smiled seeing Stavros there.

"Need any help?" Liam asked softly. He stretched with a yawn and walked into the kitchen.

Stavros glanced over his shoulder at Liam and nodded "You can set the table." he replied with a smile.

Liam nodded and got out some plates and got some glasses of juice onto the table. "I'll go get Ashton up." Liam said. He walked up the stairs and knocked on Ashton's door. "Hey lazy butt breakfast is almost ready" he called through the door.

Ashton groaned as he heard the knock on the door and slowly stood up. He yawned as he pulled on a clean shirt and clean pants and opened the door, "You're a lazy butt." he grumbled. He headed to the bathroom while Liam headed back downstairs.

Ashton joined his father and Liam a few minutes later. They all seemed way too tired to talk about anything so they ate in silence and then cleaned up the dishes. Ashton thought about just going back to bed but it was Sunday today and he didn't want to waste the weekend sleeping all day.

"Can Liam and I go to the mall today?" Ashton asked. He finished cleaning the counters and looked over at his dad.

Stavros thought for a few moments and sighed. He couldn't keep the boys inside all day.

"Yes, you two can go." he said. "But be home by supper." he added quickly.

Ashton and Liam agreed quickly and took off to get their shoes on and ran out the door before Stavros changed his mind.

Stavros sighed and shook his head with a light chuckle. He walked to his office and decided to do some work but he didn't even get three feet into his office before his cell rang. He checked the number and answered it.

"What's up, Tyler?" he asked, then winced hearing yelling in the background.

"Oh nothing much. Just dealing with an angry Dan." Tyler sighed. "He is about to be kicked out of rehab if he doesn't get his anger under control but I doubt that will happen."

"You could always actually *help* him instead of just being there." Stavros said. He rolled his eyes and sat down at his desk "He has only been there a few days. They can't kick him out for being angry. I'm sure a lot of drunks get a little upset when they are told they can't have anymore alcohol."

"True, however, at least they don't go around punching random people and threatening to murder the next dumbass that tells him to calm down." Tyler replied. He sighed heavily, "Anyways I thought you might want to know about this because if Dan gets kicked from this rehab he'll go back to drinking like crazy and Liam will go into the system since his mother is being a worthless bitch."

"Liam can't go into the system." Stavros sighed out. He knew Ashton would freak if that happened and Liam would just fall apart. Stavros knew the system was useless most of the time. Sure, they helped families but they also ruined families. Stavros would try keeping Liam under his roof but he doubted it would be allowed. Stavros wasn't family but he supposed he could always call in some favors… he did know a few people who could pull some strings.

"The system would just ruin Liam. Just.. calm the man down and fix things. He has to finish that rehab. It's only for two? Three? Months?"

"Two months. It only goes longer if he drinks while here but I don't see that happening since he isn't allowed to leave the grounds until he leaves."

"Two months doesn't seem all that long.." Stavros murmured.

"It's the typical amount. They can be in here for up to 90 days." Tyler replied. "But everyone seems hopeful that Dan will only need two months so that's what they are trying for. Right now it doesn't seem like that'll be long enough but once he actually gets over the withdrawals and such he should mellow out."

"Than you keep him there until that happens. If he tries threatening anyone else, or even goes to punch someone, knock him out. Okay? Liam has so much faith in this working that he doesn't need to be disappointed if it fails. Don't let it fail." Stavros ordered.

"Fine. I'll put in more effort." Tyler sighed. "I'll call-HEY!"

"Liam's doing okay?" Patrick's voice suddenly asked.

Stavros rolled his eyes, "I am capable of taking care of a child. I don't know if you noticed this or not but I have actually raised one."

"Only for ten years. That doesn't count."

Stavros narrowed his eyes as he tried thinking over this logic. "How many kids have you raised? Cause last time I checked you don't have any kids."

"Well not that I know of anyways. Chances are I have a million right now and it's my great genes that raises them well."

"I can't lower myself down to your level of stupidity." Stavros said. "How you managed to live this long is amazing."

"Tyler takes great care of me." Patrick chuckled.

Stavros rolled his eyes, "Liam is fine and alive. I hadn't realized you cared so much."

Patrick snorted, "I don't care."

"Than you're asking... ``why?"

Patrick sighed heavily, "Well no one would trust me to watch their little creatures if word got out that one died... duh."

"Little creatures?" Stavros repeated slowly. "I think that's one of the nicest things you've ever called children."

"For some weird reason parents get upset when I call them 'little pest' or 'rodents'."

"No really?" Stavros said sarcastically. "Who would think that was something rude to call a child?"

"Hey, have you ever met Killian? He calls them worse. Remember when Jaded actually had to shove him away from literally kicking a child through a window? And that was because it laughed." Patrick pointed out.

"Oh, how can I forget.. I had to listen to those two argue about it for five hours afterwards." Stavros groaned. "I had to actually ban Killian from going anywhere near a child... he still refuses to come to my house because Ashton is still, and I quote, "too young to tolerate." Good thing he can't stand females almost as much as he can't stand children because his kids would be screwed." Stavros sighed. Some people weren't meant to be parents and Killian was definitely one of them, Patrick was a close second. How anyone got convinced that letting Patrick watch their children was a good idea was beyond him.

He heard a beep on his phone and looked at the incoming call. "Pat, I gotta go. Liam's fine." he hung up before getting an answer.

"Ashton?" he asked, once he answered. "What's wrong?"

"Dad, you gotta come to the mall." Ashton sounded panicked.

"Why? What's wrong?" Stavros asked again.

"Liam is freaking out. Just come quick okay?" Ashton hung up before getting an answer.

CHAPTER SEVEN

"What happened?" Stavros asked, as soon as he got out of his car and ran to Ashton in the mall. Stavros had no idea what was going on but he spotted Liam and he looked to be physically okay. No blood anywhere, no wounds...

"She was here." Ashton said softly.

"She ...?"

"Liam's mom" Ashton whispered. "She saw Liam and just freaked out over nothing!. I guess she got a call from the rehab place, or from Dan, I have no idea, but she knew he was close to being kicked out of it and she just went off on Liam."

"Where is she now?" Stavros growled out. He didn't care if she was a female he wanted to tare her apart. Why did she ever bother to keep Liam if she seemed to hate him so much? He had no idea why she seemed to hate Liam, he never asked, it wasn't his place to ask, but she shouldn't be freaking out like this. It wasn't like Liam had control over this.

"She isn't here." Ashton said. "She was screaming so loud that security came and pretty much had to drag her out of her. She kept saying it was Liam's fault that his father was going through all this. She would have slapped him if I hadn't had stopped her."

Stavros cursed and walked over to Liam. The poor boy was sitting on a bench with his head in his hands just shaking and he didn't even look up when Stavros sat down beside him. He didn't say anything, he just pulled the boy close and held him. He could hear Liam sobbing but he knew there wasn't any words of comfort, not right now, not with Liam being a total mess right now. He'd have to wait for Liam to calm down before the boy would actually listen to anything he said.

Ashton stood off to the side and felt like hunting the bitch down and just screaming at her. He had no idea what her issue was but she had no right to just freak out like that.

"Is he okay?" a soft voice asked behind Ashton. He turned and looked at the female who spoke. He didn't know her all that well but he knew her name was Helliana and she was in his history class at school. She stood at 5'3, had fiery orange/red hair and gray eyes that had a tint of blue to them. She was thin, pale, and only 16 but she already had a well formed body and her skin looked so smooth. Yeah, Ashton has had a crush on her for almost three years. He had almost asked her out a few times but most of the time he couldn't even form a simple 'hello' to say to her.

Ashton opened his mouth to speak but it felt like his tongue swelled up three times its size, his throat closed, and his mouth went dry. How could this happen? Why did this have to happen?

"H-h-he um…his mom.." He stumbled over his words. It wasn't this hard to form words!

Helliana tilted her head as she looked at Liam. She vaguely knew them from her history class but she didn't talk to any of them. She honestly didn't talk to anyone. She had friends but even they got annoying to listen to most of the time. She didn't care about who was dating the hottest guy or girl around, or who messed up on a test or who's parents were being unfair. It never mattered to her and all her friends seemed to be stuck up most of the time. She didn't even pick them for friends, they just flocked over to her and never left.

"Are you okay?" She asked. Her voice was soft and sounded so much like an angels… or so Ashton thought anyways.

Ashton nodded slowly.

"Ashton?" Stavros called out softly. He stood with Liam and kept an arm around him as they walked over to Ashton and the girl. "I think it's time we go home." Stavros stopped beside Ashton and looked at the girl. He didn't know who she was but judging by how stiff Ashton was and the faint blush on his cheeks, he assumed Ashton had a crush on her. "Who is this?" he asked, a slight smirk on his lips.

Ashton cleared his throat some, "Oh, this is um… dad this is…"

"Helliana." She giggled softly. Oh jeez she had such a cute giggle! And such cute dimples when she smiled.

"Mr. Stavros. I'm Ashton's father." He smiled, and extended his hand.

"It's a pleasure meeting you." She said, shaking his hand. "Is Liam alright?" she asked softly.

"He's fine. Just had a rough day." Stavros replied. "Well, Ashton, we should head home. Helliana it was nice meeting you." he smiled. He started walking slowly with Liam and glanced back at Ashton.

Ashton waved shyly at Helliana "Bye." he murmured and quickly caught up to his father and Liam.

"See you at school!" She called after him, before walking off.

"So who is that?" Stavros asked, a grin on his face.

Ashton shrugged some, "She's a girl in our history class."

"Ashton's in love with her." Liam chuckled weakly.

"Oh?" Stavros grinned more. "Does she know that?"

"Shut up, Liam. I'm not in love with her.. I just like her.. She's a nice friend." Ashton grumbled, though he could feel his cheeks heating up.

"A nice friend that you never once talked to?" Liam teased.

"Oh, good god.. You've never talked to her?" Stavros sighed. He reached up and rubbed his temples. "I've failed as a father. How can my son not know how to talk to a girl?"

Ashton rolled his eyes. "Shh! Both of you. I know what I'm doing… you gotta build up to it."

"For three years?" Liam laughed weakly. At least talking about this made him feel a little better though his mother's words still screamed in his head.

"Why does it take three years of build up?" Stavros asked. He found this highly amusing.

"It's like foreplay.." Ashton sighed. "You can't just jump into things you have to do it slowly.."

"I realize you are sixteen but I really don't want to think about my son and the fact that he knows how foreplay works so let's just stay clear of that topic for now." Stavros grumbled. "Wait, Patrick isn't the one who taught you that stuff right?" Stavros asked, narrowing his eyes. He stopped at the car and Liam slipped in while Ashton sighed.

"No, dad, weirdly enough there is this funny class in school... what was it called? Not English.. Math? No that doesn't sound right. Oh yeah! It's called sex Ed. They kinda teach that stuff.." Ashton frowned.

Liam laughed in the car.

Stavros kept his eyes narrowed for a minute. He knew Patrick always made his little sick jokes or decided that a very detailed picture was needed when talking about his fun sex times and he also knew that Patrick would not at all care how old the person he was talking to was.

"Fine. Get in so we can go home." Stavros said. He'd drop it. He knew sex Ed was taught in schools.. It seemed odd that foreplay was involved but then again they were in highschool. He knew little pricks in high school always talked about their stupid little sex adventures. Ashton chuckled as he sat in the back beside Liam and they murmured to each other while Stavros got in and drove off to his house.

Ashton walked beside Liam once they returned home and started heading upstairs after removing their shoes and hanging their coats. It hadn't started snowing yet but it'd only be a few days before it started.

"Ashton." Stavros said, stopping both boys. "Why don't you go upstairs and Liam will join you in a minute." he smiled some. He put his shoes away and hung up his coat. He waved Liam over to him and sighed as he placed a hand on his shoulder. "I don't know what your mother said, I don't need to know. What I do know is that you are a smart young man and are handling everything with amazing strength. Don't listen to her, okay? She doesn't know what she is talking about and she has no right to go off on you like she did. She may have given birth to you but she is not your mother. She has no idea what she is missing but one day she will be sorry for not being involved in your life." he said softly.

Liam smiled weakly "Thanks. I'll try okay?" he promised. He wished he didn't get so upset over it but having his own mother yelling about how useless he was, did hurt.

"Good. Now you go up and bug Ashton while I start supper." Stavros said. He gently hugged the boy and watched as he ran up the stairs. He sighed and shook his head as he walked to the kitchen and started making supper.

"What did he want?" Ashton asked, when Liam walked into the room.

Liam smiled some, "He just wanted to help me feel better. Basically just said my mom's a bitch and doesn't know a thing about me so she can't judge me. Just in more and nicer words." he chuckled.

"Ah. Well it's true." Ashton murmured. "Anyways I saw this new game come ou-"

"No, no. We are not doing that stuff. We are going to talk about Helliana. Dude, it's about time you tried asking her out." Liam cut in. He sat down on the bed and sighed, "You shouldn't put it off forever."

"I can't even say 'Hi' to her. How the hell am I supposed to ask her out?" Ashton muttered. "She doesn't even like me. I mean we've been in her class forever and she's never even noticed me until today."

"We haven't been in her class forever. Stop being a baby. If you aren't man enough to try talking to her in person why don't you just try talking to her online instead?" Liam suggested. "It can't hurt."

"What am I supposed to say?" Ashton asked.

"How about you start with 'Hey' and see where it goes from there?" Liam smiled.

"I'm not even friends with her on anything."

"There is the school app. Talk to her on that."

Ashton narrowed his eyes some but walked over to his laptop and flipped it on. He muttered to himself as he logged onto the school app and scrolled through the names.

"That is going to take hours. Just search her name. See? Search bar. Right there!" Liam pointed to it, having gotten off the bed to stand beside him.

Ashton rolled his eyes as he searched her name and clicked on it to send a message. He tapped his fingers a little on the keys but didn't type anything yet.

"Oh for the love of.. Move." Liam scrowled. He quickly pushed Ashton out of the way and began typing.

"Hey!" Ashton snapped.

"See it's not so hard saying that to me. You should try saying that to her but maybe with a little less attitude." Liam chuckled. He sent the message and just shook his head as he listened to Ashton groaning behind him. "Relax. If we waited for you to grow the balls to do this we'd be waiting for years." Liam said with a grin.

"I hate you." Ashton muttered.

"Hey look. She messaged back. She says hi and everything." Liam said triumphantly. He began typing again and hummed softly to drown out Ashton whining behind him. He found it amusing that Ashton freaked out over such a little thing but he couldn't really give him too much trouble over it simply because he hadn't even tried getting to know his little crush.

"Why did you send a winky face? That just makes me seem like a tool." Ashton growled some. He was not enjoying this. Not. At. All.

"It shows interest." Liam explained. "You want to give this a shot?" he asked. He didn't bother waiting for Ashton to say anything though, he was really focused on the task at hand. Ashton needed a date. "Hey have you given any thought about the annoying school dance for Christmas?" he asked.

"No. Why would I?" Ashton asked. He didn't dance. He had no idea how to dance. Why would he want to go to a dance?

"Well you just asked Helliana to go with you so you might want to think about going."

"What? Are you insane? I can't dance!" Ashton gaped out.

"You might want to learn…" Liam chuckled. "Dude, she actually said yes!" he laughed. "Man you are screwed now."

"Oh I hate you. Why would you do this to me? I'm going to end up stepping on her feet or tripping her and breaking her back… oh I'm never going to get another dat- wait? She said yes? She said yes!" Ashton smiled wide. He was excited that she said yes! She actually said yes! A female had agreed to go to a dance with him… and now he suddenly felt sick. Being so excited yet nervous all at once was not a good feeling. He groaned as he sat on his bed, "This is the worst yet best thing to ever happen to me." he whispered.

"Calm down. We'll figure something out okay?" Liam said, glancing back at him.

"Do you know how to dance?"

"Um no, but I'm not going so I don't gotta learn."

"Why aren't you going? You can't make me go alone!"

"You aren't going alone, remember? You're going with Helliana. Your date. I'm not going because the rehab is closed for the holidays so my dad is coming home for a few days. Tyler promised me that he'll be in great shape for it. I'm trying not to get too hopeful about it but I'm hoping at least a little." Liam said with a shrug. "So I'll be at home with my dad. Patrick and Tyler will be there for a few hours when he first gets home and they already cleared out any booze from the house and will be keeping his money so he can't go out and by more. If everything goes great he might not even need to go back to the rehab center." Liam smiled. He had to keep reminding himself not to think too much on it or else he'd just get filled with hope. He wanted to hope it all worked out but Tyler had warned him that it might take more time than planned. He knew it wasn't something that was going to happen over night or even in a few days but just thinking about his dad sober… he remembered the few times his dad had been sober. The first time was when he was eleven and they went camping. He learned how to fish and they had a blast but that had been his first and only time to ever go camping. His father got sober again when Liam was thirteen and they went to the zoo for the first time, which was great fun, but as soon as they got home his dad started drinking again. His dad had been sober a few other times but that only lasted for a day and the whole time his dad either slept or freaked out over everything because he was craving a drink but had no money for anything.

"That's great. I hope it all works out." Ashton smiled. He really did. Sure Dan was an ass but if he got sober and actually stayed sober maybe he'd turn out to be a great dad?. It was something Liam really deserved and Ashton wasn't sure how well things would go if it all failed. He knew his best friend would be crushed.

"I do too." Liam said softly.

"Boys, come down for dinner." Stavros called up. He walked into the kitchen and sighed softly as he sat down.

Ashton walked down the stairs and into the kitchen followed by Liam. They both sat down and started to eat away at the beef stew.

Stavros was lost in thought as he ate away at his stew. The two boys talked to each other but Stavros didn't pay any attention to it right now until he heard Liam speaking to him.

Stavros looked up at the boy, "What?" he asked

Liam frowned some, "You okay?" he asked.

"Yes." Stavros replied with a sigh.

Liam chuckled softly, "We were talking about the winter dance that's going on at the school. Ashton's got a date!"

"Liam!" Ashton groaned. He stood up to bring his bowl to the sink.

"A date?" Stavros asked. He looked over at Ashton, "Who?"

"That girl, Helliana. You met her at the mall." Liam said. "Now Ashton is being all pouty."

Stavros rose a brow, "Pouty? For having a date to a dance? I thought people pouted when they didn't have a date? Man how times have changed.." he said. "What's the problem, Ashton?" he asked.

Ashton rolled his eyes, "I'm not being pouty, okay?. I am actually really excited for it." he said.

"But...?"

"But what?"

"It sounded like the end of that sentence had a 'But' in it." Stavros said. He stood and brought his dishes to the sink and glanced at Ashton as he stood beside him. "So?" he prompted.

Ashton sighed, "The dance is in three weeks.. I have no idea what I am even suppose to wear" he said.

Stavros chuckled lightly, "A suit?" he suggested. "That always seems to be the best choice. We can go out and get you one." he said. "Do you have a date, Liam?" he asked over his shoulder.

Liam shook his head, "Nah. I don't do dances." he said.

"Why not?"

"They are loud and full of stupidly annoying people." Liam stood up and brought his bowl to the sip as he sipped at his juice. He smiled some as he leaned back against the counter and finished his juice. He licked his lips and set his glass down, "Don't worry. I have no interest in a silly dance."

Ashton narrowed his eyes at Liam, "Why were you so concerned about me going than?" he asked. He crossed his arms over his chest and huffed some.

Liam snorted, "You have a girlfriend." he shrugged.

"I got a girlfriend when you played me and asked her to the dance." Ashton pointed out.

"I'm confused." Stavros interjected, before Liam could respond. "Liam got a girlfriend?"

Ashton sighed, "No… well yes… sort of.."

"Those are the three options.." Stavros said slowly.

Liam chuckled, "I used his school account to talk to Helliana for him to ask her to the dance. It's his girlfriend. I just got them talking."

"Ah" Stavros said.

"Ashton not having a suit isn't even his biggest problem though." Liam said.

"Shh." Ashton hissed out.

Liam ignored him. "He doesn't know how to dance."

Ashton glared at Liam but the boy only smiled in return.

Stavros chuckled softly as he shook his head, "That's an easy problem to solve."

"How?" Ashton asked. "I don't know anyone who can teach me to dance."

Stavros smiled, "Yes you do."

"Who?"

Stavros smiled again and gave a playful bow, "Me, silly."

Ashton stood shocked while Liam burst out laughing.

CHAPTER EIGHT

"So what are you going to do?" Patrick asked, looking at Tyler. They sat in a small bedroom in the rehab center. Dan was busy getting sick in the bathroom because he had bribed someone to bring in whiskey for him the night before. The room had a single bed, a small dresser, nightstand, and the bathroom. It was painted in gross pastel colors that made Patrick want to stab himself in the eyes with a rusty fork. Patrick wore a blue short sleeve shirt with black slacks and orange running shoes.

Tyler sighed heavily, "I have no idea." he said. Tyler was dressed in a dark blue suit though he looked so uncomfortable in it.

"Are you going to tell Stavros?" Patrick asked, a slight smirk on his lips.

"Hell no." Tyler growled out. He didn't have to report everything to that man and he honestly didn't want to listen to the guy whine about all of this.

"So what's the plan?" Patrick asked. He knew Tyler had to have some sort of a back up plan.

Tyler shook his head as he heard Dan throw up again and wrinkled his nose in disgust. Why would anyone be willing to get drunk if it caused them to be sick the next day? He didn't understand it. "We are going to take him home." Tyler finally answered.

Patrick choked and stared at Tyler, waiting for him to actually explain his suicide plan. "What?" he finally asked, when Tyler remained silent.

"We will take him home and just deal with all this there." Tyler said. "He got kicked out, it's not like we can just hide him here." Tyler sighed. Why did he bother dealing with this? He should have just stayed hidden away.

"What about Liam?" Patrick asked. "I thought we were suppose to be 'helping' them. You know how bad things can get with Liam there and plus Stavros will end up finding out."

"You scared of him?" Tyler asked with a smirk.

"You aren't?"

Tyler sat there for a minute and actually thought about that. He had many reasons to fear Stavros but the man wasn't like how he used to be. He actually seemed to...care. Which was sickening and made him seem a lot less scary. "I am scared of him but not as scared as I use to be." Tyler askered.

Patrick snorted a laugh and shook his head, "Not at all comforting."

Tyler ran his fingers through his hair, "It's not suppose to be comforting." he sighed. "I can't convince the annoying fat head to keep Dan here." Tyler did not like the lady who ran this place, Trish, because she acted like everyone was beneath her and she shit gold. He already got into a few arguments with her.

"Well I guess you can get him all packed up and bring him back home. I'll leave and go get Liam." Patrick said. He stood up slowly and stretched, "How will we keep Liam from saying anything?" Patrick asked.

Tyler shrugged as he stood up slowly, "That is something for you to figure out. Now go before Dan leaves the bathroom and starts a fight with you again."

Patrick rolled his eyes as he walked out the door. He already got into two fights with the man over nothing. Dan seemed to just get pissed off anytime Patrick opened his mouth to speak.

Patrick walked out to his black mustang and muttered to himself as he got in and took off driving. How the hell was he supposed to figure this out? He growled under his breath and clenched his jaw every so often as he tried to think of something.

Tyler finished getting Dan's things together and knocked on the bathroom door, "Dan?" he called out. "It's time to go."

Dan let out a groan but said nothing.

Tyler cursed under his breath and forced the door open. He looked at the pathetic human lying on the bathroom floor covered in sweat and even vomit. He fought the urge to roll his eyes as he knelt down and looked him over, "You're a mess."

Tyler grabbed the man's arm and yanked him up onto his feet as he stood and kept a firm grip on his arm to keep him from stumbling back. He walked Dan out of the bathroom and forced him to sit on the bed. Dan was 5'9 with short blonde hair and had the same blue eyes as Liam.

Tyler worked on changing Dan into a clean shirt, happily the man didn't try fighting against him, and put the dirty shirt into the garbage. He sighed softly as he looked the man over and shook his head, "Lets go." he murmured. He honestly wished he didn't have to deal with such things sometimes.

Tyler walked out of the door with Dan's bag and glanced back just to make sure the idiot was actually following him. He looked bored as he watched Dan stumbling behind him and had the sudden urge to punch him but such things could wait until later he supposed. He didn't need or want Dan bleeding all over his car.

The walk out to the car felt like it lasted for hours, since Dan seemed to have trouble remaining on his feet or even walking a straight line, but Tyler refused to help him any. Tyler got the bag into the trunk of his silver jag and opened the back door for Dan so he could at least lay down and sleep the whole car ride. He got the man buckled in and shut the door, even made sure the child safety lock was on, before he got into the driver's seat and took off to Dan's house. Tyler knew he'd have to clean it out of any alcohol, even though he didn't really care if Dan went out to buy more, and he'd have to stay close to the house to see how things went. Dealing with drunks was annoying to him but things were going so perfectly with Dan and Tyler knew it wouldn't be long before he got a decent meal.

"I don't think it fits right." Liam said. He was at a tailors shop with Ashton and Stavros to get a nice suit all fitted for Ashton.

"It's itchy." Ashton grumbled. He was not a fan of this at all. Why did he have to wear a suit? Wasn't jeans and a shirt good enough?

"Relax, Ashton. It looks great." Stavros said. "You are taking a lady to a dance and you have to make sure everything is perfect. It's a big deal for you and her so relax and let the man do his job. He is almost done anyways."

Ashton muttered to himself and just stood there as the tailor made adjustments on the black suit.

"Alright. I got what I needed. You may change into your clothes but don't knock out the pins or I'll have to do it all over again." The tailor said. He walked over to his desk and started writing things down.

Ashton got off the stool and practically ran to the change room. He knew his father mentioned getting a suit but he hadn't realized he would have to actually do it. He shut the door and carefully removed the suit and set it to the side neatly, just to make sure he didn't knock out any pins, and then changed into his own clothes.

Liam slowly paced around the room and looked at all different kinds of fabrics and suits hanging along the walls. The room was in the back of a suit shop just for fittings. It had a red carpet with brown walls, a wall mirror between two dressing rooms, a desk full of papers and a computer, and another door to the bathroom. Liam ate an apple as he walked around and tried not touching anything since Stavros already warned him that he'd get broken fingers if he did.

"How long until it's ready?" Stavros asked the tailor.

"It should be less than a week. I'll give you a call when it's done."

Stavros nodded and waited for Ashton to exit the dressing room. He thanked the tailor and walked out of the store with Ashton and Liam close behind him. "Alright so that's all done. Should we get some lunch?"

Liam tilted his head, "I would but that looks like Patrick." he pointed ahead of them.

Sure enough it was Patrick.

Patrick walked up to them and stopped a few feet from Stavros, "Hey, Stavros." he greeted.

Liam smiled as he stepped forward, "How's my dad doing?" he asked, before Stavros could say anything.

Patrick shrugged, "As good as expected I guess. I've come to take you home now."

"Home?" Stavros asked before Liam had the chance.

Patrick gave a nod, "Yes. Tyler and I have decided it was time to get Liam back on a normal routine so I will be staying with him at his house and he can go back to school tomorrow."

Liam was excited about that, sure school did suck but he didn't want to fall too behind on his school work.

"Well I guess I'll see you tomorrow at school." Ashton said with a smile.

Liam nodded and moved to stand beside Patrick, "What about my stuff at Ashton's house?"

"He can bring it to school tomorrow for you." Patrick replied.

Liam nodded and waved bye to his friend as he followed Patrick out to his car. He got in and smiled as he looked at Patrick, "So what's all going on with my dad?" he asked.

Patrick sighed as he started the car and began to drive, "You'll find out soon enough," he murmured.

CHAPTER NINE

"Why is he home?" Liam practically yelled. He had arrived home with Patrick and discovered that Tyler was back with Dan instead of at the rehab center.

Patrick sighed as he sat on Liam's bed while the boy paced around the room. Liam's bedroom was painted a pale blue and had posters of random things hanging on the walls. He had a single bed with a nightstand beside it that looked like it'd burst apart if touched and a small desk that was messy on top.

"He got kicked out of rehab so Tyler decided to bring him home and try helping him here. Tyler cleaned out any booze laying around and he will be staying here until Dan is able to be alone." Patrick explained.

Liam shook his head, "It's not going to work with him being here. He has to go somewhere else."

"Do you have the money for that?"

Liam stopped moving and glared at Patrick, "You guys paid for it once. Why can't you do it again?"

"We aren't made of money" Patrick replied. It was a lie but Liam didn't need to know that. "Just calm down, Liam. Take deep breaths and make yourself relax. It will be more difficult this way but it can work."

Liam rubbed his face and sighed heavily as he flopped down on his bed. He stared at the wall for a few minutes "Why can't I stay with Ashton? Or at your place?" he asked softly.

Patrick shrugged, "I'm suppose to be watching you, not pawning you off to someone else, and we weren't planning on telling anyone about Dan."

"Why not?"

"Because something like this isn't going to work if everyone knows about it and comes poking around every five seconds." Patrick explained with a sigh. Why did he have to explain things to a teenager? Couldn't he just sit down and be silent while doing as he is told?

"I'm not supposed to tell anyone?"

"No. Right now Tyler is working on Dan and we don't need Stavros coming here and yelling about all this so for now just keep it to yourself."

Liam gave a nod and sighed. He didn't like keeping anything from Ashton. They were best friends and told each other everything but he knew he had to keep this to himself for right now.

Patrick watched Liam for a minute before he stood up and left the room. Things were working out perfectly so far and he knew it wouldn't be much longer before they were ready.

Liam was nervous about all of this and how it'd actually go but he had to have some faith that everything would work out. He knew his father wasn't some horrible guy when he was sober, he was actually kind and encouraging and they did things together.

Liam listened to his father yell at Tyler and bit his lip. He hoped a fight didn't happen. He didn't hear Tyler so he assumed the man was talking. Could this actually work? Did he dare hope it would? He has been let down in the past… Liam shook his thoughts out of his head and decided he just needed to shower and get to sleep and that's exactly what he did.

It had been two weeks since his father returned home and at first everything had been fine. Tyler stuck around and helped his father cope with no alcohol and his father was even getting better. Liam had been so happy and his father even seemed happy, he praised Liam on his good grades and was actually acting like a real father. Liam had still kept it a secret that his father was home even though it was hard. He wanted to tell Ashton how great things were going right now but Patrick kept insisting that Liam remain quiet about it.

Liam had spent a lot of time over at Ashtons right after school to work on homework and laugh his ass off watching Stavros trying to teach Ashton to dance.

It was a week before the school dance and Ashton still wasn't getting the hang of how to do anything.

"Why do I even have to learn to dance?" Ashton grumbled. They had moved things around in the living room so they had an open floor and could dance without bumping into things.

Stavros sighed, "Because you are taking a lady to a dance."

"Yeah but kids these days don't actually dance. They just stand around talking and laughing." Ashton said.

Stavros rolled his eyes as he sat on the couch to take a break. "You are getting better at this. You just have to stop being so tense and stop stepping on my feet."

"You have huge feet. If they were a normal size I wouldn't step on them so much. Helliana has normal feet. I'm not at risk of stepping on them."

Liam laughed, "Might want to warn her to wear steel toe shoes."

Ashton glared over at him as he crossed his arms over his chest. "Haha. Very funny."

"Shall we try this again?" Stavros asked. He stood up and held out his hand to Ashton.

Ashton groaned but took his father's hand and put his left hand on Stavros' waist. He was trying to learn how to lead the dance this time. He muttered to himself and stepped forward but ended up stepping on Stavros' toe and tripping over him. Stavros was quick to catch Ashton before he face planted on the floor.

"You guys aren't even listening to the right music. I'd just like to point out that kids these days don't really do the waltz or any of that stuff. They pretty much just grind against each other." Liam said with a chuckle.

Stavros released Ashton and stepped back from him, "I'm not teaching you that and you better not be grinding against her." His eyes slowly narrowed as he spoke.

"This is all your fault, Liam. Had you just left it all alone I wouldn't be in this mess right now."

Liam laughed at Ashton's words, "True. You'd be pouting because you would be staying home and not going to the dance with the girl you really like."

Ashton opened his mouth to speak but was silenced when Liam's cell rang. Liam pulled his cell from his jeans pocket and answered.

"I won't be grinding against her, dad." Ashton said, turning his attention to his father. "If she wants to dance I'll dance with her but she won't be mad if we end up just standing on the side and talking instead."

Stavros shook his head slowly, "Schools shouldn't do a dance if no one dances at it. What's the point?"

Ashton shrugged, "None of the kids seem to complain about it so why bother stopping?"

"I have to go." Liam said. He walked to the front door and pulled on his boots and his coat. There wasn't a whole lot of snow on the ground, maybe an inch or two, but Liam got cold so easily and he knew his toes would freeze off if he didn't wear winter boots.

"Something wrong?" Ashton asked.

Liam shook his head, "No, I just need to get home. I'll see you in school tomorrow." he said. He waved bye and quickly ran out of the house before anymore questions were asked. His father was the one who called him and Liam had no idea what was going on but he was worried. His father was yelling about something and right now Tyler was getting groceries and Patrick had left a day ago to take care of some other business. His father didn't sound drunk so maybe something was actually wrong? It had always been hard to understand his father when he yelled because he'd jump all over the place with his words and be calm for a few seconds before going back into a raging fit.

"Dad?" Liam called out, walking into the house. He removed his coat and shoes as his eyes looked around the house. It seemed quiet right now… Liam walked towards the living room but stopped hearing something behind him. He turned and let out a startled cry when something hard collided with his stomach. He fell to his knees gasping for breath and already felt tears fill his eyes as he looked up and saw his father's angry face staring down at him. It was in that moment that Liam realized his father reeked of whiskey. He was drunk and Liam knew it was about to be much worse when his father's left arm lifted into the air with a belt clenched in his fist.

CHAPTER TEN

"I want him to die" Liam whispered. He had given up on believing his father would get sober and be a real dad to him. He was curled up in the bathroom, new bruises covered his arms, back, and stomach. He rubbed his eyes and shivered a little before he gasped out, nearly jumped out of his skin when he looked up and suddenly Patrick was sitting there on the side of the bathtub. "How the hell did you get here?" Liam demanded.

"You called me." Patrick replied, a small grin on his face. "So I came."

Liam narrowed his eyes "I never called you." He quickly stood up and grabbed the bathroom door handle and turned it but Patrick was up and keeping the door shut with his hand in an instant.

"You did call me. Your sorrow called out and I answered. I feel your pain, know your rage, I'm here to make your desire come true." he purred softly, his face inches away from Liam's.

Liam felt his breath catch in his throat and he wanted to scream, he was panicked, but the way Patrick was staring at him was almost.... calming, in a way. He watched those eyes go from the normal hazel to a flash of yellow, then returning to the normal eye color. "What are you?" Liam heard himself whisper out. He wasn't sure he'd want the answer.

Patrick smirked darkly and stepped closer to Liam. He ran his fingertips over Liam's cheek slowly "I'm a demon" he purred. "I'm here for you, to help you get your dark desires." he whispered. "I'll take away those that cause you great pain." he purred, an evil grin on his lips.

Liam stumbled back away from Patrick, his face holding the look of horror and his breath catching in his throat once again as his back hit the wall. He just stared, unable to find his voice as a thousand thoughts ran through his mind. Was it seriously true? Maybe some kind of sick joke? "You're lying" he heard himself whisper out. No way this was actually true.

Patrick tilted his head slowly and held back a chuckle "Lying? Why would I lie to you?" he asked. "I get to fill out your dark desires, you can't hide them from me. I know what they are. I know who you want revenge against, I know you want to make those suffer the way they made you suffer." he purred. "You will not act on them yourself, so I get to do the dirty work."

"For what? my soul." Liam growled out. "Why would I agree to shit like that? What makes you think I'd want that?" Liam hissed.

Patrick grinned and watched him for a moment, his eyes flashing the sickening yellow, as if peering into Liam's soul. "You may not agree to it now but in the end someone always becomes desperate enough to take on the deal. A soul is worthless to you, its filled with sorrow, fear, hate, and pain, and yet those are the sweet flavors that one, such as myself, craves." he licked his lips at the thought of tasting his delicious soul.

"Oh so I get sweet revenge but then get to burn in hell? Sounds like some sweet messed up deal" Liam rolled his eyes. He couldn't believe this was actually a conversation he was having. Maybe he was having a horrible dream? There was just no way this was real.

Patrick laughed softly and shook his head "Who ever said you'd burn in hell?" he smirked. "Your father is not going to change. Those bullies at school are not going to change. You will be beaten and tormented by them everyday until you are pushed to do the unthinkable. A human soul can only take so much until it finally snaps and that raises the question on how much you believe you are capable of taking before you finally snap?"

Liam swallowed roughly "I'm strong enough to take it.." he whispered. He didn't believe his own words and it showed.

"For how long? Months? Years? You'll reach your moment of breaking and do the unthinkable and waste such a perfect soul" Patrick replied smoothly.

Liam looked away, his breathing felt heavy to him "What is unthinkable?" he whispered, though he knew he already knew the answer to that question.

"Such a silly question to ask." Patrick said. He moved over to Liam and gently grabbed the boys chin to make him look up into his eyes "Every soul gets to a horrible point in its life, some are strong enough to push past it but others give up all hope and when that happens they decide death is a lot more welcoming than life is and so they end it." he replied.

Liam's eyes widened as he stared into the demon's eyes. He felt a scream catch in his throat, terror filled him and he quickly had to push the demon out of his way to throw up in the toilet "You're lying" he gasped out. He gagged and spit, trying to regain control of himself to stop from throwing up again.

Liam heard the demon chuckle behind him "As I have said, I have no need to lie. What you saw is true. Think of my offer, I can be of great service to you and when you decide to use me simply call out my name." The demon whispered beside Liam's ear before he simply vanished in yellow smoke.

Liam clung to the toilet, as if holding onto it for dear life. He couldn't forget what he saw, couldn't even find the words to speak of what he saw. He didn't want to believe it but in those demon's eyes he saw it and part of him knew it would become true. In those sickening yellow eyes he saw himself, body limp on the ground, foam all over his mouth, eyes wide open and lifeless with an empty pill bottle beside him. Liam swallowed hard and stood on shaky legs, he turned on the water and washed his face before he looked in the mirror and stumbled back with a small sob escaping him. He saw his lifeless body in the mirror and he knew it had to be true. He saw his own death caused by his own hand.

Liam stumbled from his bathroom and into his room. He couldn't sleep, the hours of night ticked by but he couldn't even shut his eyes for a minute. He couldn't stop trembling, couldn't stop crying. He kept seeing his dead body over and over again, how had Patrick shown him that? What if it wasn't true? What if the demon was just trying to get his soul? Why did a demon even need a soul? He had so many questions running around his head but he had no answers. He stayed on his bed, holding his knees tightly to his chest and stared at the floor as his mind went in a whirlpool of thoughts.

"You should have waited longer before telling him the truth." Tyler said, standing beside Patrick. The two men stood on a rooftop across the street from Liam's house. It was nearing two am so it was still pretty dark out.

Patrick put his hands in his jeans pockets and shrugged lightly "I could have." he smirked. "But his emotions are already high up there. He's almost perfect to feed from, soon I'll have his mind snapping with insanity." he licked his lips. He couldn't wait to devour such a tortured soul.

Tyler rose a brow and glanced at him sideways "Take care, brother. You push things to fast with him and it won't be as you want it. Snap him too much and he'll no longer be your dinner."

"Oh shut up." Patrick hissed. "You get the father, why are you bitching about this? You've already twisted Dan's mind. I would have thought you would have collected him by now."

Tyler smirked and licked his lips "Oh don't worry, I'll be tasting his blackened soul soon enough. The only hold up we have is getting permission."

"I never knew you as someone who actually waited for such things. What is it everyone always says? Better to ask for forgiveness than permission?" Patrick chuckled. "Wait, don't tell me, little baby is scared" he fake pouted.

Tyler rolled his eyes and shoved him "That is how the saying goes, however, for the one we would ask for forgiveness from, it's highly unlikely he would give it. Everyone knows he doesn't like others feeding on his land, I don't blame him. He has juicy souls here, it just happens to be our luck that the emotions running through Liam and Dan are not to his taste." he pointed out. "Besides, we'll get our answer tomorrow. Until then, we wait."

"I hate waiting" Patrick groaned. "It's like having to wait for foreplay to end in sex. Why men bother to waste time on such a useless thing is beyond me. Who cares if the chick enjoys it? Personally, I hate foreplay, as long as I enjoy myself and reach the end I don't care how she feels about it."

"It always amazes me how we go from talking about souls, to you mentioning something about sex. Damn, by now I have a clear imagine in my mind how you do sex from all the crap you mention. I know, foreplay is beyond you, but have you ever thought that maybe, just maybe, it might be more enjoyable if you actually knew what you were doing?" Tyler said with a sigh. Oh he was getting a headache now, he really wished Patrick was quiet but sadly he was never that lucky.

"What? are you offering to teach me such skills? Oh great master?" Patrick joked and smirked.

Tyler narrowed his eyes "Am I the only one who knows we are brothers? Has that information slipped your mind?" he growled in disgust.

Patrick smirked as he shrugged "What? We share souls sometimes, is sharing a woman really that different?"

Tyler shuddered "Oh you are sick. Yes, dumbass, sharing a soul is so far different than sharing a woman. I don't have to see your naked ass, for one, and they are both filling in their own ways."

"I thought you did the filing with a female?" Patrick was enjoying himself.

"I need to bleach my ears out." Tyler shuddered again. "I know you like to do sick jokes but please, for me, leave me out of them for now on so I don't die from vomiting." he groaned. He rubbed his temples and stepped back from Patrick "I can't believe you are my brother... you act like a damned child."

Patrick rose a brow "How many children do you know-"

"I take that back!" Tyler cut in. "I don't need to know what you were about to say. I'm sure it was far from pleasant. I'm going to the hotel to wait for an answer. You do as you please, just... do it far from me." Tyler turned and walked off. He knew by now he really shouldn't be surprised by all the crazy crap his brother said, but he still got shocked by some things.

Patrick chuckled under his breath as he glanced back and watched as Tyler faded away. He rolled his eyes some "Big baby." Patrick crouched down as he watched the house, he couldn't see what Liam was doing but he could feel everything happening to him. "Soon, little pet, you'll be ready." he purred. He licked his lips and turned as he stood to walk off. He knew his brother was right, they couldn't feast until they got the OK but at this point, whether he got the ok or not, he was going to enjoy that boys soul.

Ashton had been trying to reach Liam for days. He hadn't seen him at school, at first he thought he was sick, but even when he'd try to text or call him, he heard nothing back. He stopped by a few times after school but no one ever answered the door. He was starting to get really worried, it wasn't like Liam to miss so many days of school without at least texting to complain about being sick or whatever was going on.

Ashton rubbed the back of his neck as he walked into his house and kicked off his shoes. He tossed his backpack on the ground and glanced at his phone once more. Nothing. "Where are you Liam?" he whispered. He rubbed his forehead as he walked to the kitchen to get himself a glass of orange juice.

"Is something wrong?" Stavros asked.

"Jesus!" Ashton jumped, sighing as he spilt some juice all over the counter. "Damn dad, don't sneak up on me like that." he sighed.

Stavros chuckled "A little jumpy, are we?" he asked. "Don't tell me you did something stupid that will end up with you getting into trouble?" he asked. It'd explain why he was jumpy.

Ashton cleaned up the juice and tossed the cloth into the sink "No." he sighed once again. "It's Liam... he hasn't been at school in a few days and he isn't answering his phone or door... I'm just worried. It's not like him." he murmured.

Stavros frowned as he crossed his arms over his chest and leaned against the doorway "How long has it been since you last heard from him?" he asked curiously.

"Um..." Ashton rubbed the back of his neck as he thought about it. "We are on Thursday? I think Saturday night or Sunday was the last time I talked to him.." he said.

Stavros growled quietly and glanced out the back door. He narrowed his eyes slightly for a second before he sighed "I'll call his mother and see if she's heard anything from him.." he said. He knew the truth, but he wasn't about to tell Ashton it.

"Even if he is at his moms, he still would have at least sent a text. He's my best friend, we haven't gone a day without talking since we were like… seven. The only time we don't talk is if we're grounded." Ashton replied.

Stavros pushed off the wall and sat down at the table "Well maybe he got grounded."

"Grounded from school too?" Ashton asked. "Highly unlikely. That's like you grounding me and not letting me go to school."

There was something wrong, Ashton knew it. He knew there was no way he'd be missing school if he was just grounded, plus, even with his father being off the booze, grounding wasn't a punishment the man used.

"He could have gone to see his father."

Ashton shook his head, "He still would have sent me a text."

"You're right." Stavros sighed. "I'll make some calls while you start on homework." He stood up from the table and walked to his office. He shut the door and growled under his breath. Stavros walked to his desk and picked up his phone, he already knew who he had to call.

"You can't stay locked in your room all the damn time! Damnit, Liam, don't make me break the fucking door down." Dan yelled from the hallway. Tyler was sitting on the couch in the living room just smirking as he sipped at his coffee.

"What a troublemaker he is." Tyler smirked. He set his coffee down and licked his lips. "He's already missed four days of school. What if he misses more?"

"I'll beat his ass black and blue if he does." Dan snapped. He paced the living room and shoved his hands in his pockets "What the hell is wrong with him? He ain't dead." he growled.

Tyler felt his phone vibrate in his pants pocket but he ignored it. He stood up slowly and watched the man pace "No, I think he's just showing so much disrespect towards you." he grinned. "Man, I'd flip shit if my child acted this way towards me. What do you think he's doing up there?" he asked.

"I don't want to leave my room." Liam whispered. He had hardly moved from his bed ever since Patrick showed him his future.

"You can't stay in bed all day, what if your dad comes storming in here?" Patrick murmured softly. He sat on the foot of the bed and watched the boy. "You don't need to fear me, Liam."

"You're a demon. What's there not to fear? Are you going to be giving me chocolate and pop? Or a car? No. I doubt that. You only want my soul" Liam whispered. He glanced at Patrick and swallowed roughly "Why do you even want it?" he asked.

Patrick smirked "I could give you many things however with your state of mind, having you drive a car is a very bad idea. A body can live without a soul, it's not like you'll be dead without one, you'll just be..." he paused as he thought of the right word to use. "Empty, in a way. Taking your soul would be painless and, honestly, you won't even miss it." he purred.

Liam frowned "Empty.." he whispered. How would that feel? Would he really care? Or would he not even notice?. "You haven't answered why you want it."

Patrick smirked and licked his lips "A demon's gotta eat. You'll be dead in a few years anyways, why care what happens to your soul?" he asked.

Liam shuddered "What will happen if I die without a soul?" he wasn't sure if he really wanted an answer to that question.

Patrick sighed, already annoyed with the questions. He always got annoyed with the questions. Why did people get so worried about their souls? The only use they seemed to have was feeding a demon. "Nothing happens. You just die. Even with a soul, when you die. You're dead. I don't know if people are teaching that heaven and hell crap, or if they now have new names for them but either way, nothing happens. There is no bright light at the end of the tunnel, no angels calling out to you, no reaper leading you to the other side." Patrick enjoyed being a demon, he enjoyed all the lies he got to say but he wouldn't start telling the truth now.

"You can't keep pacing back and forth and bitching about everything." Tyler sighed. "You are making me feel sick. Instead of staying down here, why not have a few more drinks? Or better yet, grab that belt and beat some sense into your annoying child. It's not like he's willing to leave his room." Tyler smirked once again. Oh this was always his favorite part. Most demons worked alone, but him and Patrick, well they didn't fight for the same food. Tyler liked his bitter, Patrick enjoyed his doused in sorrow. It's why it worked so well working with him, they both knew how to push the right buttons to make their food snap.

Dan curled his lip as he snarled "Fucking child. If he won't come out on his own, I'll drag his ass out." he spat. He finished off his whiskey, slammed the glass on the table and stormed up the stairs after he grabbed his belt. He didn't bother to knock on the door, he kicked it, hard, and watched as it broke off the hinges and fell to the floor.

Liam wiped his eyes and looked at Patrick "Can you really help me?" he asked.

"Of course."

"Against everyone? My dad, the bullies…"

Patrick smirked as he stood up slowly. "I am a demon. There isn't much I can't help you with." he purred.

Liam opened his mouth to speak but ended up jumping when his door was kicked in. He went wide eyed as he watched his dad storm into his room and let out a cry when the belt struck him on his side. He heard his father yelling about something, felt more of the hits, but it all faded as he looked up at Patrick.

Let me help you, Liam. You can't do it on your own.

Patrick's voice spoke in Liam's head, he couldn't speak. He couldn't breath. He knew his father was still hitting him, heard him yelling about something but everything seemed like it slowed down. He watched Patrick, trying to decide if getting his help was the right choice.

Patrick rose a brow as he kept his eyes on Liam. He didn't move to stop Dan, he didn't care to. The more the boy got hit and yelled out, the better his soul would taste. Patrick smirked darkly when Liam gave him a nod. "Oh goody" he purred. "Tyler" he purred out.

Tyler flashed into the room and chuckled darkly. The room darkened as Tyler's brown eyes turned white. His fangs grew larger and he caught Dan's arm before he landed another blow on the little pest on the bed.

Dan turned to look at Tyler and went wide eyed. Just as he opened his mouth to speak, Tyler yanked Dan forward and sank his fangs into the males shoulder. He shivered with delight as Dan fought, Tyler loved when they fought. Tyler chuckled deep in his throat as he ripped away from the males shoulder and licked his lips "Oh so tasty" he purred. He licked his lips again and watched the male fall to the floor. Tyler wasn't done just yet, he crouched down in front of Dan and grabbed his chin "So twisted. So bitter." he grinned. Tyler grew his claws out and plunged them into Dan's chest, he squeezed his heart and shut his eyes as he grabbed Dan's soul into his hand. He ripped his hand free of his chest and licked his fingers slowly "Such a lovely taste. I'll be full for a long time." he laughed.

Liam stared in horror. He couldn't speak, hell he couldn't even scream or think straight. He was frozen on his bed and had no idea what horrified him most. His father's dead body on his floor, or the demon covered in blood by the body.

Patrick moved over to Liam and lightly stroked the boys hair "Don't worry, my pet. He won't hurt you anymore. No one will." he purred. "We can't stay here, little pet." he reached down to grab Liam's hand and looked at Tyler. "I'll see you in a while." he smirked. He knew Tyler enjoyed playing with blood. Patrick didn't wait for Liam to speak, he flashed them both out of the room to leave Tyler alone.

Stavros cursed as he hung up and rubbed his temples. He growled and glanced at the clock. With a sigh, he stood and walked upstairs to Ashton's room. He knocked and opened the door slowly, smiling some seeing the boy passed out on the bed. He sighed and covered him with the blanket before he shut off the lights and shut the door as he left the room.

Stavros glanced around the hallway and grumbled to himself as he walked to his room after locking up the house and went to bed.

"Dad" Ashton whispered, shaking his dad softly. "Dad!" he nearly yelled after a few minutes.

Stavros opened his eyes and groaned as he sat up, "Ashton?" he glanced at the time. "It's 3am. What are you doing awake?" he asked.

Before Ashton could answer a loud knock sounded on the front door again. Stavros tensed as he stood and walked out into the hall "Wait here." he ordered.

He walked down the stairs and turned on the lights as he unlocked the door and opened it. He blinked as he looked at two cops standing on the porch.

Mr. Stavros?"

"Yes?"

"I'm officer Kyle Skilts. I have the understanding that you were close with Mr. Tase and his son Liam?" the officer said.

"Liam?" Ashton said, standing at the bottom of the stairs. "Yes. Why? What happened?"

"Ashton, please." Stavros said, looking over his shoulder at him. He was worried now. He turned his attention back to the officer at his door. "Yes"

Officer Kyle let out a slow breath "May I come in?" he asked.

"Yes." Stavros said, as he stepped back to allow him inside.

Officer Kyle stepped inside and shut the door behind him and gestured for Stavros to take a seat on the couch.

Ashton watched from the stairs as they walked into the livingroom and then quickly ran down the stairs to stand in the doorway.

Stavros glanced at Ashton and grumbled under his breath "You might as well come sit down here, Ashton." he sighed.

"We had a call a few hours ago." officer Kyle started. "We arrived at the house and found the body of Mr. Dan Tase-"

"What about Liam?" Ashton asked. He felt his heart quickened at the thought of him dead as well.

"We haven't found him." Kyle explained slowly. "We found his body in Liam's room, Mr. Tase is dead and we are not sure where Liam went off to." he said softly.

Ashton choked back a sob and stared at the officer for a few minutes trying to figure out what he was saying. He heard his father speaking but he did not hear a word he said.

Stavros was surprised to hear that Dan had been home and even mentioned to the cop that they had both thought Dan was still in rehab.

Liam cleared his throat and shook his head "You think Liam did it." it wasn't a question.

Officer Kyle tensed for a moment before he spoke "We asked around about the family. We checked out his moms house but he wasn't there. She informed us that Mr. Tase was an abusive drunk. We understand in cases like these the victim can snap and lose control of their actions."

Ashton shook his head quickly "Not Liam. His father was getting help. My dad paid for his rehab! He was getting help and Liam was all excited about it and was even making plans for them to just move on from the past and they were going to be happy and father and son again and.. And.. and Liam wouldn't do this!" Ashton wouldn't believe it. He couldn't. Liam was his best friend and the most gentlest person he ever knew! It wasn't in Liam to kill his father. Hell the boy wasn't even able to kill a spider!

"Ashton." Stavros said calmly. "Do you know where Liam is?" he asked.

Ashton shook his head again "I-I-I don't um.. I don't know.. He hasn't been answering my text or calls.. He hasn't been in school for a few days.. He.." he felt like the world was spinning. What if Liam was dead too? What if these asshole cops were just assuming Liam killed his father? "What if Liam is missing? What if whoever got his father took him to?" Ashton whispered.

Officer Kyle shook his head "If Liam hasn't been in contact with you it has nothing to do with his father's murder. That happened a few hours ago. Liam could be in danger and we have to find him. Do you know where he might go?"

Oh, of course Ashton knew many places Liam could go to but he was not about to tell them any of that. "He could have gone anywhere. He could have gone to his mothers or maybe he could have gone under the bridge where a lot of kids like to hang out." Ashton spoke quickly. He couldn't get his thoughts straight, he couldn't wrap his head around all of this. How could he? He had been worried about Liam enough as it was and now… now he was wanted by the cops and missing? How could that be possible?.

Stavros watched the pain going through Ashton and reached over to take his hand "it's okay, Ashton. We'll find Liam. He couldn't have gone far." he said soothingly. Stavros looked at the cop, "He could also be with Patrick and Tyler Linval." He said. He told them where they were staying.

Japher nodded quickly "We'll find him" he whispered.

"If you do happen to find him please call me or bring him to the police station." Kyle said as he held out his card to Stavros. "I'm very sorry for your loss" he said as he stood.

"Losing Dan is nothing" Ashton whispered. He had no love for that man. "We just have to find Liam. He wouldn't have done this. I don't care what you assholes think! Liam wouldn't have done this." Ashton snapped.

Stavros stood "Ashton." his voice was stern. He took the card from Kyle and set it on the table. "I'm sorry officer Kyle" he said as he walked him to the door.

Officer Kyle shook his head "Don't be. I know this must be hard for you and your son. We need to understand what happened at Mr. Tase's house and we need to find Liam. We don't know if he is injured or if he is the one who caused his father's death. We need to find him" he whispered softly.

Stavros nodded "If we find him we will call you" he assured. He opened the door and rubbed his face as the officer walked out to his car and drove off. Stavros closed and locked the front door before he returned to the living room and sat down beside his son. "Are you okay?" stupid question..

"No" Ashton whispered. "They think Liam killed his dad. He wouldn't have done it. I know he wouldn't have done it. He couldn't have. He was so excited! So excited for his dad to get clean! He went on about it for hours. How could this happen? What if Liam got hurt? What if he's dead?" Ashton choked as he tried breathing and talking all at once. He gripped his hair as he rested his elbows on his knees and placed his head in his hands.

Stavros rubbed his back slowly "Deep breaths, Ashton. Don't think about that okay? Just keep telling yourself that he is fine and alive. We'll find him. I don't believe he killed his father and I'm sure once we find him we'll all learn the truth" he said softly. He stood to grab his phone and sent out a text then looked back at Ashton "It's getting close to four in the morning. Why not go upstairs and try sleeping for a few more hours okay?" he suggested. "We can't go out right now to look for Liam. It's late and dark outside, we'll never see him." he added.

Ashton opened his eyes to stare at the ground and remained silent for a few minutes. He didn't want to sleep. All he wanted to do was go out and look for Liam but he also knew his father was right. It was too dark outside and they'd never find him right now. He knew a few spots Liam could be in but they both had one favorite spot they always went to but that involved the cliffs which wasn't really safe to go around during the day let alone at night. "Okay" Ashton finally whispered. He stood without another word and went straight to his room. He's feet felt so heavy and his mouth was dry while a million thoughts ran through his head. He heard his father's voice call to him but he couldn't hear what he was saying.

Stavros sighed as he watched Ashton go to his room and then glared at his phone when it rang. "What did you do?" he snapped as he answered it. He walked to his office and shut the door behind him "What do you mean? 'Nothing?' I know you've done something so stop blabbering and spill it already." he growled. He growled loudly as he listened to the voice and rubbed his temples "I told you no. Do you remember that? You were both supposed to pick up and leave but instead you decided to not listen and do this shit anyways? What were you thinking?" he hissed. "Stay away from Liam. Stay away from

Ashton. Pack your shit and get out of here. Now." he spat and snapped his cell shut. He let out a slow breath to calm himself and then walked over to his desk, sat down, and began doing some work on his laptop.

"Please don't be dead." Ashton whispered. He had tried calling Liam seven times already but he got no answer. He threw his cell on his bed as he paced his floor and rubbed his face. "This can't be happening. How can this happen?" he whispered. He pulled out a black shirt and blue jeans. He wasn't sitting around anymore. He quickly changed and grabbed a flashlight and his cell. He left his room and quickly ran down the stairs to get his shoes on.

"Where are you going?" Stavros asked, walking towards Ashton slowly.

"I can't sit here and wait. I have to find him. I can't leave him alone." Ashton said. He got his shoes on and looked at his father "I'm going whether you want me to or not so you can either come with me or just sit here but I'm going." He yanked his jacket from the closet and reached for the door.

Stavros cursed under his breath and grabbed Ashton's arm "*We* will go together. Let me change quickly and then we will go." he said. He knew this was probably a bad idea but he couldn't let Ashton go alone and he knew his son was going to do it anyways.

Stavros wasted no time changing and once he made sure he had his wallet, cell, and keys, he headed out the door with Ashton. He locked up the house and glanced at Ashton, who looked like he was so lost in deep thought, "Do you know where he would go?" he asked softly. He knew Ashton didn't tell the officer everywhere that Liam may have gone.

Ashton shrugged weakly "He could have gone to the cliff. We like hanging out there at times… he could have gone under the bridge or even to Alex's house.."

Stavros nodded and got into his car, "We will look for a few hours but do not get panicked if we don't find him."

Ashton gave a nod but he had no idea if he'd even be able to that. He had so many things running through his mind right now and he couldn't sort any of it out no matter how hard he tried.

CHAPTER ELEVEN

It was near 9 in the morning when Ashton and his father returned home. They had no luck finding Liam and he still wasn't answering his cell. Ashton tried not thinking of the worst things possible but it was hard and the longer he didn't hear from Liam, the harder it was to keep positive. Ashton went straight up to his room and plugged his cell in to charge before sitting on his bed and rubbing his face. He was exhausted and knew he had to get some sleep but part of him was afraid he'd wake up to knocking on his door and finding out that Liam was found dead somewhere.

"You doing okay?" Stavros asked from the doorway.

Ashton shook his head slowly but didn't speak.

Stavros frowned as he walked into the room and sat down beside him, "We'll find him. Okay? You need to try getting some sleep now and when you wake up we'll get something to eat and good looking for him again." he promised.

Ashton gave a weak smile, "Okay" he whispered. He stared at his cell for a few moments but when nothing happened he just laid down on the bed and sighed heavily.

Stavros stood slowly and watched Ashton for a minute. He knew this was hard on the boy and he knew they needed answers. Stavros pulled the blanket over Ashton and shut the door as he left the room. He went to his own room and called Ashton's school to explain why Ashton wouldn't be there then got himself settled into his own bed to sleep.

Ashton woke up five hours later to the sound of his cell vibrating. He rolled over to grab it and sat up quickly when he opened the message and saw it was from Liam.

I'm okay. Don't look for me.

It's all the message said and Ashton read it about a thousand times. He tried calling Liam and sending a lot of text but he didn't get any answers. He growled in frustration and walked to his window. He stared out it, half hoping that Liam would be standing outside waving at him to come out but there was nothing but morning traffic. He glanced at the date on his phone and sighed seeing it was the seventeenth of December. The school dance was in two nights and he knew there was no way he was going to it if they hadn't found Liam by than. He had been so excited, nervous, but excited, to go and now he couldn't even focus on it. Ashton sighed and decided it was best to just take a shower and eat some food so he could take time to clear his head and talk with his dad about the next plan. He knew if Liam didn't want to be found he wouldn't be in his normal hiding spots. Ashton heard some banging in the kitchen and assumed it was his father making some food but he ignored that for now and grabbed a towel from the hall closet and took his shower.

Stavros decided to make some bacon and eggs with some toast when he heard the shower running. He knew Ashton needed to get a bit more sleep so he hoped eating would make him tired enough to sleep but he also knew that Ashton was worried about Liam and wouldn't be focused on anything else except going off to find him. Stavros had tried calling Patrick and Tyler but none answered which was starting to piss him off but at the moment he knew he couldn't do anything about that. Stavros just finished putting the food on the table when the shower turned off and a few minutes later he heard Ashton leave the bathroom. He sat down and sipped his coffee and was joined by Ashton a few moments later.

Ashton sat at the table and poked at his eggs with his fork. He was starving and knew he had to eat but the thought of eating also made him feel sick. "Liam sent me a text." he said softly.

Stavros blinked, "Oh? What did he say?"

"That he is okay and not to look for him."

"Do you believe him?"

Ashton sighed and set his fork down, "I honestly don't know. I don't know what to think about any of this. I didn't even know his dad was home from rehab. Liam doesn't normally keep things from me and I can't understand why he didn't tell me this. I just.. I want to know what's going on with him and what happened."

Stavros nodded, "Well if he doesn't want to be found we won't find him."

"I can't stop looking for him.." Ashton said, frowning.

"I'm not saying to stop looking for him. I'm saying just take the rest of today to calm yourself down and think about some places he'd going hide at so he can't be found."

Ashton didn't like the idea of just sitting here and doing nothing but his dad was right, he had to think of spots Liam would hide in to keep from being found. He would assume Liam would hide at his moms but he knew Liam would never run there because his mother would kick him out or call the cops first chance she got.

Ashton pushed away from the table and headed up to his room to try and get a little more sleep. He lay on his bed for almost twenty minutes before he decided he wasn't going to get any sleep so he went to his laptop and pulled up a map of the area. He had heard on the radio earlier that it was supposed to be a bad snow storm tonight so he wanted to try finding Liam before that happened so he didn't freeze outside.

Stavros cleaned up the kitchen when Ashton left and went back to his office. He sighed as he checked his cell and sent another message out to Patrick. He knew it was useless though because the man wasn't going to answer him, especially if he had Liam with him.

"Dad?" Ashton called out softly. He walked down the stairs, "I think I know where Liam might be.. Normally we'd go hide out by the cliffs but if he doesn't want to be found he could be hiding out past them and around the waterfall."

Stavros stepped out of his office and gave a nod as he listened, "We can look there." he replied. "Get ready to go. If we can't find him there then we'll just hang out here until tomorrow."

Ashton nodded and prayed they found him there. He tried not dwelling too much on what happened at Liam's house because he'd end up with more questions than answers and it'd drive him insane.

Ashton pulled on his blue winter coat and boots, there wasn't much snow on the ground still but it was colder out now, and headed outside with his father following behind him.

Stavros knew this was going to be a waste of time but he wouldn't stop Ashton from looking and he wasn't about to let him go off alone.

It was just under thirty minutes when Stavros pulled up to a parking lot and turned the car off. There was a large cliff in front of them and a few shady stores beside them across from the cliff. One store was a pawn shop, which was closest to the cliff, and had boards up on the store window since someone had thrown bricks at it a few weeks back. A clothing store was connected to the pawn shop but it was going out of business so it had a lot of 'for sale' signs around to get rid of the leftover clothing still inside. A used book store was beside that but it had been broken into a week ago by some punks who decided to set a bunch of books on fire so it was still getting fixed up. This wasn't an area that Stavros liked his son being in.

Stavros got out of the car and walked beside Ashton up the path to the cliff and stopped at the tree line. Since it was winter there wasn't any leaves on the trees but they were really close together and went out into a large wooded area that was actually easy to get lost in. Most teens loved hanging out in the woods and causing all kinds of trouble but rangers started going through the woods at random and threatened to fine anyone they saw so it did help to keep people out of the deeper parts of the woods.

Ashton sighed and shivered just a little from the cold breeze as he walked on the trail towards the falls. He looked around the whole time he walked just hoping he'd catch sight of Liam. He heard the low rumble from the falls just ahead of them and remembered the first time he and Liam went there. It was an early summer morning and they were about ten years old. They had saw deer walking through the woods that day and heard all the birds singing, smelt the flowers and grass. It was really beautiful and they even went swimming at the falls. The water came down from a mountain, well they called it a mountain, in truth, it was just a massive rock hill. They never went to the top but near the bottom was a pond that was great for swimming and even fishing at the right time of year. They had went back there many times after that day.

Stavros stopped beside Ashton and sighed as he looked around slowly but he saw nothing and all he could hear was the water flowing under a small sheet of ice. Stavros glanced down at Ashton and saw the hope get crushed in his eyes but there wasn't anything he could do about that. "He isn't here."

Ashton shook his head, "He could be somewhere.."

"Ashton." Stavros said firmly. "There is no place around here that would keep him warm. He'd end up freezing. He wouldn't come out here before a snow storm." he explained.

Ashton wanted to scream in frustration but he knew it'd solve nothing. He could spend hours looking everywhere around here but he knew his father was right, Liam hated the cold and wouldn't be out here even if it was to hide. He gave a nod and followed his dad back to the car.

CHAPTER TWELVE

Tyler watched from a leather red chair as Patrick paced around the livingroom and tilted his head, "How's it going?"

The living room was painted a dark blue and had a bright red couch along the far wall with a glass coffee table in front of it. The floor was hard wood but it did have a checkers pattern rug in the middle of it. There was a bookshelf in the left corner and a 60' TV in front of a large window that was hidden by black curtains.

Tyler wore a pair of black jeans and a white shirt that had two blue stripes going across it.

Patrick had just thrown on some black sweatpants and didn't bother wearing a shirt which showed off a small tattoo on his left shoulder blade of the head of a dragon that breathed fire. The fire was red but the dragon head slowly turned colors to show what kind of demon he was. His Lord was the demon of emotions, there were eight different races of demons, and they were all unique in their own ways. Patrick loved tortured souls to feed on, he always went for a human who was a victim of some form of abuse and loved to play with their minds. Tyler had always gone for the abuser because he enjoyed bitter souls, it's why they both worked great together.

"It's going fine. Or at least if would be if Liam would stop crying and panicking about all this." Patrick grumbled.

"I told you not to push him too much too fast." Tyler replied. "You could have very well ruined your supper."

Patrick stopped pacing, "He isn't ruined. He just needs to be reminded of why he asked for my help."

Tyler chuckled, "I don't think that is the problem. I think all he is remembering is how you helped him."

"Shut up." Patrick hissed. "You're the one who killed his father right in front of him."

"You told me to."

"I didn't tell you to do it right in front of the boy."

Tyler stood slowly and stretched, "True but you could have easily taken him somewhere else. Now stop playing with your dinner. Cops are everywhere and soon we are going to be hunted as well."

"Human's have no chance of finding us."

"I'm not talking about the humans." Tyler growled. "We went against orders. You know we weren't supposed to feed on these lands but we did anyway and now we need to just hurry up and leave so we don't end up dead."

Patrick crossed his arms over his chest, "You are a huge coward for a demon.."

Tyler narrowed his eyes, "I'm not a coward. You know who he is and what he is and we have no chance of beating that."

Patrick shook his head and walked out of the room towards the stairs, "Yeah, Yeah. Whatever." he called over his shoulder. He headed up the stairs and stopped at the first door on the left. He knocked on it three times, "Liam? You can't stay hiding in there all day."

Patrick waited a few moments and just flashed himself into the room when Liam didn't answer. The room was dark and only had a bed in it which was were Liam was. He was curled up on the bed just staring at the wall in front of him.

Patrick held back a groan of annoyance and stepped forward. He crouched down in front of the bed and looked at Liam for a moment, "Are you planning on snapping out of this any time soon?"

Again no answer.

Patrick wanted to strangle him. He lightly tapped Liam's head "Anyone alive in there?"

Liam swatted Patrick's hand away, "Go away."

"Oh my Lord, he spoke!." Patrick gasped. "Here I thought the cat did catch your tongue."

Liam rolled his eyes, "What?"

"You know that stupid saying? 'Cat got your tongue?'"

Liam just sighed and shut his eyes.

"You can't be going to sleep.. We have things to do, remember? Those bullies aren't gonna lay down and die just for you."

"Go away." Liam muttered again.

Patrick frowned as he stood up and tilted his head. He looked at the pathetic human over slowly and sighed.

Liam had the blanket over his waist and legs and wore a grey shirt. His hair was all messy and his body was still healing from some bruises. Patrick could heal the wounds but he didn't want to. Liam also now had a tattoo on the left side of his neck, it was the same one as Patrick's. It was a way for a demon to show who the human belonged to. Not all demons marked their food but Patrick wasn't risking some other snot nose demon coming along and stealing his hard earned meal. A demon could kill a marked human but they couldn't devour the soul, only the owner of said human could do that.

Patrick reached down to grab the bedframe and quickly jerked it up to flip the bed over. He chuckled hearing Liam gasp and then curse as he hit the wall behind him and fell to the floor. Liam kicked the blanket and mattress off him to glare at Patrick.

"Oh good. You're up. Now come down stairs and get plotting your revenge against those horrible bullies like a good little bad guy so I can kill them and then leave."

Liam flipped him off as he stood and muttered to himself as he walked down the stairs and slumped down onto the couch. He was struggling with grasping everything that was going on at the moment. He was with two demons and one had killed his father a day ago, or was it two days? Maybe a week ago? He had no idea anymore. He had tried asking questions about the demons but they didn't seem happy about answering questions, in fact they had been real annoyed and threatened to remove his tongue many times. He was told the cops were looking for him and he had wanted to call Ashton just to explain what happened but Patrick had taken his phone and told him not to worry about that stuff right now.

Liam had gathered some information when he heard Patrick and Tyler talking last night but all he found out was that they needed to leave town quickly before the demon Lord in this town found them. He guessed they were doing things against the rules or something. When Liam first came here he spent the first few hours getting sick and when he found out the cops were looking for him, wanting to question him about his father's death, he broke down and cried for a while and begged Patrick to fix everything that had happened. It was Tyler who snapped at him about being weak and that his father had been a good meal and he should stop crying like a baby. After that Liam spent most of his time lying in that bed and ignoring the outside world.

"Finally he honors us with his presence." Tyler mused.

Patrick leaned against the doorway and half shrugged, "He wanted to be a baby about it but I snapped him out of that."

"I am right here." Liam hissed.

"Do you think he'll start crying again?" Tyler asked. "Because that was real annoying."

"I hope not. I might have to remove his eyes to stop it if he does." Patrick replied.

Tyler chuckled, "That could actually be fun. You should try that.. Maybe we can spoon them out.."

Patrick shook his head, "Why use a spoon? I got claws, that'd be a lot more fun to use."

"That is true."

"I.AM.RIGHT.HERE." Liam snapped. "And you can't spoon my eyes out."

Tyler glanced over at Liam and slowly rose a brow, "I could too. You aren't much of a fighter, it'd be so easy."

"Leave him alone, Tyler. He's grumpy." Patrick sighed. "How do humans stop being grumpy?"

"We could try hitting him really hard…"

"Dan did that a lot and it didn't seem to help."

"What about sleep?"

"No, he's had enough sleep.. Food?" Patrick suggested, looking at Liam. "Are you hungry little pet?"

Liam clenched his jaw and counted to ten to keep from snapping at the morons. "I'm not a pet." he hissed through his clenched teeth.

Patrick shrugged, "You are pretty much. I have to feed you, take you on walks, make sure you get sleep and have a bath.."

"I can do that all by myself."

"Fine."

Liam stood up and walked to the kitchen and fought the urge to punch Patrick as he walked past him. He opened the fridge and blinked seeing it was empty. He started opening cupboards and saw they were all empty too. "Do you have any food?"

"I thought you could do this all yourself?"

Liam slammed the cupboard shut and tried weighing his options. He could always punch Patrick but the guy was a demon so that would likely end up with him losing his hands. They did not like it when people spoke loudly around them so screaming at them was a bad choice too.

Liam let out a real slow breath, "Can you just answer the question?"

"We don't have food because we don't eat food."

"How did you plan on feeding me if you have no food?" Liam snapped.

Patrick shrugged, "There's a burger joint down the street.."

"Which would work great if I wasn't currently being looked for by the cops."

"He has a good point." Tyler interjected. "He can't leave here until you two are ready."

Patrick let out a heavy sigh, "Fiiiiiine." he dragged out. "I'll just go get him something than. What do you want, Liam?"

"I don't know."

"Fries? Pop? A burger? Seven burgers?"

"Nothing... I'm not hungry."

"Than why the f-" Patrick growled and clenched his fists. "Why ask about food if you don't want anything to eat?"

Liam shrugged, "You flipped the bed over on me so it was my turn to annoy you."

Tyler laughed, "You two are a messed up married couple."

Liam sat down on the couch again and crossed his arms.

Patrick stayed by the doorway and watched Liam for a moment. His pet was being annoying but the emotions running through him was making his soul seem far more delicious that it made his mouth water. He licked his lips and just thought about how close he was to getting that yummy soul. Sure he could easily take it now but having the soul get twisted in it's emotions made it taste so much sweeter.

"So now we work on a plan to get those bullies and we have to do it tomorrow night." Patrick said. He knew it was already a high risk being here and the longer they stayed, the higher the risk.

CHAPTER THIRTEEN

Ashton stood in a dark corner of the room just listening to the rain pounding against the cottage. He saw someone sleeping in bed but the boy quickly woke up hearing screams. Ashton looked towards the door and waited to see who would come through the door. The boy on the bed had crawled off it but didn't move towards the door, instead of curled up behind a trunk. Ashton had this dream before. He knew any moment now a dark figure was going to walk through the door and take away the boy. No, not a dark figure, a man. A man was going to save the boy. This dream felt so familiar to him but why? He knew this room.. He knew this house was located in the middle of the woods but he didn't understand this dream. He watched the door to the bedroom open slowly and watched the man walk into the room. He looked like someone he knew. The man spoke but Ashton couldn't make out the words. He stood there and watched as the man picked the boy up and turned towards the door to leave but not before Ashton caught a glimpse of his eyes. They didn't look normal they looked black but, than again the room was pretty dark, it was the red that caught Ashton's attention. Those eyes looked so black but for some weird reason they had bright red pupils. What the hell?. Ashton stepped forward but froze when he realized something else, that boy was him. This wasn't a dream it was a memory that he couldn't fully remember. He also realized that the man who came to save him as a boy was now the man he called father.

Ashton jumped awake breathing heavily and looked around the room quickly. What was with these dreams? No, not dreams, it was a memory. Stavros didn't have those kinds of eyes though.

Ashton grumbled, "You watch way too much TV" he murmured to himself. He glanced at the clock and saw it was just after six in the morning. He hardly remembered even going to bed. He knew they looked around the waterfall for Liam but found nothing and then they came home, ate, and Ashton went up to his room. He sighed as he slipped out of bed and pulled on some clean sweats and a shirt. He ran his fingers through his hair as he headed to the bathroom and washed his face with some cold water.

Ashton headed downstairs once he finished in the bathroom and wasn't surprised to see his dad sipping at some coffee at the table while reading the paper.

"Morning." Ashton murmured tiredly.

"Good morning." Stavros replied. "Do you want some breakfast?"

Ashton shook his head and got himself a glass of orange juice.

Stavros sighed softly, "They cancelled school for today." he said. "Some kids from the school have turned up missing. Apparently they never made it home from school yesterday. Since they haven't been found and with three new murders in the last week, the school board has decided to start winter break early."

Ashton would have been happy about that if Liam wasn't missing. "I know some places have high crimes but it's odd we are getting a lot of it."

Stavros nodded, "It is. This place is normally quiet but for some reason murders are happening every other day right now. If it keeps up like this the police are going to put up a curfew."

Ashton sat down and yawned softly. He checked his phone but wasn't surprised to see no new messages. "Are we looking for Liam today?" he asked.

"We had a pretty bad storm last night so I don't think we'll find Liam out on the streets but we can try. You need to eat something first though."

Ashton nodded and stood up to get himself a bowl of cereal. He wasn't hungry enough to eat a whole lot right now.

"I heard you making some noises in your sleep. Did you have a nightmare?" Stavros asked. He had thought the nightmares had stopped by now.

"It wasn't really a nightmare it was more so just a weird dream." Ashton replied. He sat down at the table and began eating his cereal.

Stavros studied Ashton for a moment but didn't press the issue. He returned his attention to the paper and read it for a few more moments before he set it aside.

"Liam's mother has been murdered this morning. The cops stopped by asking questions again but it doesn't seem like they are having any luck getting answers either." Stavros said.

Ashton felt a cold chill run down his spine that caused him to shiver. He didn't like the woman but he knew if she was dead then the cops would be hunting for Liam even more. It seemed they already planned on pinning the blame on Liam unless they found something to prove it wasn't.

Ashton didn't speak about Liam's mother because he had nothing nice to say about it. Instead he looked at the paper and frowned as he yanked it closer to him. "Are these the guys who went missing?" he asked.

Stavros nodded, "You know them?"

"Not really…"

"But?"

Ashton sighed, "These are the four guys who pick on Liam all the time at school."

They were the jocks in the school and they all played hockey together. They were tall and had solid muscle on them. The leader, Tim, was 6' 3 and had short blonde hair with green eyes. He was a huge dick who always had some lies to tell about someone and enjoyed beating up Liam every chance he got. Some people at the school believed that Tim was homosexual as well but was too ashamed to admit it so he beat on Liam. Ashton just believed he was a dick who enjoyed picking on people for fun.

Another boy, Sam, had long black hair with brown eyes and was the same height as Tim but not as built. The guy was always quiet but had a very short temper.

Cody was an inch taller than Tim and had brown hair with blue eyes. This guy was always telling jokes and enjoyed making people laugh but he also enjoyed making himself laugh by beating someone else up.

Derek was the fourth guy and was Tim's younger brother. He had the same hair and eyes as Tim, was about two inches shorter, and was far too much like Tim. The four of them had always had fun picking on Liam. Ashton tried stopping it whenever he was around because he didn't care if they kicked his ass instead but for a while now they had managed to wait until Ashton was out of sight before they beat Liam.

Ashton and Liam had both told the principal at the school but it never helped. The bullies would be suspended for a few days or spend time in detention but that was it and when they saw Liam again they always beat him worse for ratting them out.

Stavros frowned hearing Ashton's words and knew the cops would keep looking at Liam as a suspect if things didn't change quickly. Stavros knew this wasn't Liam but he had no proof and everyone who made contact with Liam in the past was now turning up missing or dead. It wasn't looking good.

Ashton cleaned up his bowl once he finished eating and checked his cell again. He had already tried calling Liam but, like always, he got no answer. He kept picturing Liam dead somewhere. It had only been a few days since all this started with Liam but it had already been so draining and felt like it's been weeks.

Ashton headed to the front door and got his winter gear on to keep warm. He glanced back at his dad and waited for him to be ready before he opened the door and stepped outside. There were about seven inches of snow on the ground now and even though the sun was hidden by clouds, it wasn't horrible cold out.

"Where should we look first?" Stavros asked.

"We could check the mall to see if he'd go there to warm up?"

"No. Everyone knows who he is by now so he wouldn't go to the mall where he'd easily get caught."

Ashton got into the car with a sigh as he tried thinking harder about where Liam would have gone. He came up blank. "I'm not sure where he'd go."

"Well we'll just keep driving around and keeping our eyes open." Stavros said. He pulled out of his driveway and drove down the street. Ashton stared out the window watching everything they passed and hoping once again that they'd find Liam.

They drove around for hours and only stopped once to get some lunch before they went back to looking again. At times they'd stop to look down alleyways and even in some small stores but everywhere they went was a dead end. Ashton didn't want to give up but he had no idea how much more of this he could even take. How did they know Liam was still alive? They checked in homeless shelters and under the bridge but no one had any information to share.

Stavros was half tempted to just hunt down Patrick, he knew he had something to do with this but he'd have to wait until Ashton was sleeping first so Ashton didn't ask too many questions about why they would go see Patrick.

It was just before supper time and Stavros pulled up into their driveway. He turned off the car and looked over at Ashton for a moment, then got out of the car and walked up to the front door. Ashton waited a few moments but then joined his father inside the house.

He removed his winter gear and sat on the couch and stared at his phone.

Patrick smirked as he watched Liam, the boy got that angry spark back into him. They boy seemed nervous at first, like Patrick would kill him for planning the murder of four other boys, but Patrick made no move to do so. Patrick had gathered up those bullies and had them locked up in a dumpster by the cliff, they were knocked out so they wouldn't be drawing attention. He didn't feel like bringing them home and they wouldn't freeze to death as long as Liam actually did what he planned.

Tyler stuck close by them just so he and Patrick could leave as soon as Patrick had Liam's soul. They were in the woods around the cliff for right now. Liam was laughing like a lunatic and kept mumbling to himself. Tyler was listening for any unwanted guest and Patrick was staying close to Liam to whisper encouraging words.

"Come, little pet. It's time to get this over with." Patrick purred.

Liam gave a nod and walked with Patrick towards the dumpster that held the bullies.

Ashton put away the pizza his father had ordered and the wings while his father went to take a shower. It was already pretty dark outside and he had promised his dad he would stay home for the night but he couldn't.

He slipped out of the house while his father was in the shower and quickly ran down the street. He'd check the cliffs again one last time and if Liam wasn't there than he'd return home and pick things up again tomorrow.

He paused seeing a group of kids, clearly drunk, stumbling across the street and quickly walked past them. He heard them calling out to him but to his relief, they decided to leave him alone and carry on their own way.

The cliff was at the edge of town and normally took quite a while to get to from his house, since he was pretty much in the middle of town, but he knew some shortcuts and ran most of the way so he cut his time in half.

He saw something on top of the cliff and as he got closer, he realized it was seven people standing at the top. He thought about turning around since Liam didn't hang out in crowds but something inside him told him to keep walking.

Tyler was enjoying this human who fought back against him. He had planned on just staying to the side and letting Patrick have all the fun but when they got the humans up here, they woke up and tried fighting for freedom. Tyler had grabbed one of them by the throat and squeezed pretty hard, the human had gasped for breath and even tried clawing Tyler's arm off. Tyler tore into that guys throat with his fangs and sucked out his soul. Tyler didn't normally drink a human's blood, most times it was disgusting and had an awful aftertaste but this time he did drink the humans blood and didn't even mind doing it.

Tyler kicked the second male in the leg to knock him down when he went to run. He smirked and reached down to grab him but stopped hearing a shout.

"Stop!" Ashton shouted. It was Liam. He had found Liam!. He stood by a building and looked up at them.

Patrick tilted his head while Liam seemed to not even notice he was there.

"Kill him" Liam hissed at Tyler.

Tyler grinned and shoved his claws into the males stomach. He laughed as the human screamed, the other two humans were still bond so they couldn't move, and yanked out his intestines.

Ashton stood frozen as he watched what was happening. Liam actually wanted this to happen? Was Liam really the one doing all this?.

Liam looked thinner to Ashton, paler too. He just looked so unhealthy and seeing him actually laugh as Tyler killed the bullies… it was sickening. His best friend was a sweet, caring, guy. How could he allow this to happen? How could he want it to happen?

"Liam!" Ashton called out. There wasn't a way up the cliffs from here. The path up the cliff was covered in deep snow by now and was five blocks away.

Liam glanced over at Ashton and gave him a smirk but said nothing to him yet.

Tyler made quick work of the last two jocks because now that Ashton was here, doing demon things was a risk. They couldn't kill this boy… or could they? Stavros wasn't around..

"It's it time to go?" Liam actually pouted at the thought. He was actually having fun with this.

Patrick grinned, "Not yet, pet, We still have to find that last bully of yours."

Liam was excited at those words until he remembered that Ashton was there with them now. "What about him?" he asked.

Patrick glanced at Ashton and shrugged, "What do you want to do with him?" he asked.

Liam tapped his chin as he thought about that question. What should he do with him? He was getting in the way and ruining his fun time but he didn't have a chance to answer because Ashton spoke again.

"You can't do this, Liam. You have to let this go and just come with me now, please?" he begged.

Liam growled, "I can do this! I got my two demons with me and they'll make sure this happens for me. They'll set everything right for me."

Ashton was shocked. Demons? What? There weren't any demons! He had no idea what Liam was talking about. "Are you high?" he couldn't stop himself from asking.

Liam didn't answer that. He hadn't taken any drugs but was there other ways of feeling high? He thought so because at this moment he did feel high.

"Liam, please come down here and come to my house. We can fix this." Ashton pleaded. He had no idea how the hell they'd fix this but he had to try something, right?

Liam laughed darkly as he stared down at Ashton from on top of the cliff. "It's best you don't get in my way, Ashton. I don't want to hurt you but if you try stopping me than you'd give me no choice," he growled.

How did this even happen? Ashton couldn't believe what was happening and he wished he just stayed at home so he didn't have to witness any of this.

CHAPTER FOURTEEN

"Liam!" Ashton snapped out. "You can't do this! You can't use them to kill everyone who has wronged you!" Ashton felt like screaming at him, running over to him and beating some sense into him. Ashton was still trying to figure out what was even going on! Demons? What? Liam had demons working for him? How the hell did that even happen? How does that even work?

Liam smirked "You don't seem to understand that I, in fact, can. With these two helping me I can do anything! I can hurt those assholes who hurt me in the past!" He laughed once more, much like an insane person. Ashton seriously thought he was insane from how he was acting.

"Liam.. Please... Don't do this," Ashton pleaded. What was happening? How did his best friend become so... So dark? So messed up like this? "You don't have to be like them.. Things will get better." He tried to reason. Ashton was willing to try anything, he needed his best friend to just snap out of this blood lust.

"I disposed of my father and mother." Liam purred. "Now it's time to get rid of the rest of those bullies, those shit heads that ever thought it was funny to beat me." Liam nearly yelled out. "I'LL SHOW ALL OF THEM!" He screamed.

"Liam STOP!" Ashton felt tears streaming down his face. He saw the look in his best friends eyes, that blood lust, the love of having so much power, so much control, he lost his best friend. The boy he was looking up at was only a stranger to him now.

"I said get the hell out of my way." Liam snapped. "Remove him!" He snarled, turning his attention to Tyler who stood on his left. Tyler had an evil grin on his face, the air around him swirled around like a tornado was surrounding him. Tyler's clothing was already stained with blood and shredded apart along the chest and arms as if someone had been fighting back against him but clearly they lost. Blood dripped from his mouth and fingertips and his eyes were pure white but Ashton could see that Tyler was enjoying himself, he was amused and all too happy to cause chaos and suffering to someone.

Patrick hadn't said a word the whole time, nor did he move from Liam's side but Ashton realized that Patrick had actually been speaking, he'd whisper whatever bullshit words into Liam's ear. Patrick was still clean, he wasn't covered in blood like Tyler, his black shirt and black pants were still nicely kept but the look on his face.. It scared Ashton. Patrick looked at Liam like a meal, like a starving person would look at a steak and it was very unsettling.

Ashton looked back at Tyler, catching movement from the corner of his eye and then suddenly, Tyler was right in front of him. He moved with such speed that he had just been a blur, Ashton wasn't sure if he actually jumped down from his spot beside Liam on the cliff or if he simply just appeared in front of Ashton.

Ashton stepped back but Tyler quickly grabbed the front of his shirt and yanked him close. Ashton could smell the foul blood on Tyler's breath, could hear the deep chuckle leaving the demon's throat. "I'm going to enjoy this, pathetic boy" The demon hissed. Ashton could have sworn that the demon's voice was an echo, it didn't sound like a normal voice anymore. It sounded far away but the words repeated in his mind over and over again. Ashton grabbed at Tyler's arm and tried pulling himself free from his grasp but when that failed he tried hitting the male in the face, tried kicking at his legs but the demon seemed to not care about the hits, he took them like Ashton was throwing little pebbles at him, like it was nothing.

"Might as well give up, you can't win here," Tyler laughed darkly. He raised a hand, Ashton now noticing he had long horrible looking fingers, but as he actually focused on them he saw that they weren't fingers, but long claws on his fingertips. Ashton went to shout out but suddenly he felt a harsh stabbing pain on his face. He let out a cry and moved his hand up to cover his face, he felt the wetness, felt the scratches. He had to close his right eye because it kept filling with blood and burning his eye. Ashton let out a sob, not just from the pain, that he could handle at the moment even though it did hurt but seeing his best friend allow this to happen, knowing his best friend commanded this to happen, that hurt more then five lousy scratches on his face.

Ashton opened his mouth but then suddenly he felt something grab the back of his shirt and ripped him away from Tyler. At first, Ashton thought it was Patrick wanting a turn, but when he was finally released and able to regain his footing from stumbling back, he realized it was his father standing there right in front of Tyler.

"You foolish piece of filth," Stavros growled out at Tyler. "You had your fun and decided to ruin it by attacking my son?" He snarled out. He was angry. Ashton felt the air get cold, almost to the point of freezing. Stavros didn't give Tyler a chance to say anything before he shot a hand forward right into Tyler's chest. "You are done bringing terror to this world." Stavros smirked and held onto Tyler's rib cage, at least that's what it looked like he grabbed onto from Ashton' angle but really he had grabbed onto Tyler's spine. Ashton saw something shine in his father's hand and forced himself to focus on that but his left eye kept watering and he still couldn't remove his hand from covering his right eye. He was able to focus enough just as his father raised his hand and with great speed, sliced all the way through Tyler's neck. Tyler had clawed quite a bit at Stavros chest and arm, even aimed for his face before the blade, which was shorter than a sword but just a little longer than a dagger, had gone through his neck. Ashton shut his eyes tightly but he heard the gurgling sound of someone choking on their own blood. He heard Tyler trying to scream out, heard him even try to laugh and speak but he just choked on his own blood. Stavros released his grip on Tyler's spine and pulled his hand from his body and stepped back as the body went limp and fell to the ground. Stavros glanced back at Ashton but his focus didn't last long on him because Patrick let out a roar of rage.

"You son of a bitch!" Liam snapped. "Why would you do that? HOW did you do that?!" He hadn't thought something like that would happen.

"You ordered your demon to attack my son, I wouldn't just sit back and allow that to happen." Stavros replied calmly. He knew he couldn't reach Liam, the boy's mind was already too far gone. Patrick had done his work well and twisted the boys mind bad enough that the boy was even willing to attack his own best friend. "Very easily." He smirked in response to his second question.

Patrick jumped down from the cliff and lunged at Stavros but he was not as big or strong as Stavros so he was easily grabbed by the throat and pinned against a nearby building. "You really want to die like him?" Stavros growled out.

"You killed my brother, I'll kill you," Patrick snapped.

Stavros laughed and then let out a growl when Patrick shot his knee up quickly and it impacted with Starovs' lower stomach. He released his hold on Patrick and jumped back a few feet, Ashton was just watching this all happening, trying to wrap his mind around what was going on. They moved so fast but to Ashton it seemed to all move so slowly as fear of losing his father crept into his mind.

"Dad watch out!" Ashton called out. Patrick ran straight at Stavros but he didn't have a weapon, he just had long claws out and ready to rip into Stavros. Ashton took a step forward but then stopped himself and looked up at Liam, maybe he could convince Liam to stop this? Ashton watched his father for a moment with his good eye and then pulled off his dirty blue shirt. It was pretty cold out so Ashton knew being shirtless wasn't the smartest idea but he had to ignore the cold right now and get to Liam. He pressed the shirt against the claw marks on his face and then ran towards the cliff, but out of the way of his father and Patrick. He looked for an easier way up but when he was unable to find any, he took off his belt and used that to keep the shirt pressed against the claw marks. He could tell they were deep and he was a little dizzy from all the blood spilling out but right now he had to ignore it as much as he could. He knew climbing was a stupid idea because of the snow and possible ice but he had to get to Liam. He looked at his father once more and then began to climb.

CHAPTER FIFTEEN

"You honestly think you can kill me?" Stavros laughed as he jumped back from Patrick. He had a slash marks across his chest, the blood soaking through the black shirt that was shredded enough that it seemed like it was about to just fall off anyways. Patrick wasn't unharmed either, he had cut marks on his neck, shoulders, and a few on his arms. Patrick was smaller so he was faster but Stavros was smarter and quick with his knife.

"I can try," Patrick hissed out. "You aren't all powerful, there's a way to kill you and I'll figure it out." He smirked.

"Sometime before you die in this fight?" Stavros chuckled bitterly. "How foolish can you seriously be?" He growled as he lunged forward. He slashed at Patrick but he was quick to roll out of the way and stabbed his claws into Stavros' side, just under the rib cage, and earned a snarl of pain from Stavros and a backhand across the face to get knocked away.

Patrick grunted from the hit but rolled to his feet but stayed crouched down, ready to attack once again.

"You're wasting your time here. Your brother attacked my son, do you really think I'd let that slide?" Stavros hissed.

"No," Patrick grinned. "He isn't even your son though, why care about this boy who has nothing to offer you?" He questioned.

Stavros threw his long knife, smirking when it slammed into Patrick's shoulder and he let out a cry of pain. "He has much to offer me but that is no business of yours seeing as you'll be dead soon anyway."

"We'll see." Patrick snapped and jumped at Stavros again.

"Liam!" Ashton panted out, finally reaching the top of the cliff. "Please, stop this!" He coughed out. He felt like he was about to pass out. He quickly walked towards Liam, unable to run currently, and fell to his knees once he reached him. "You can stop this, please!" Ashton pleaded with him again.

Liam spun to the side, having been so focused on the fight he didn't notice that Ashton had been climbing the cliff, and narrowed his eyes. "Stop it? Why? What does stopping it do for me?" He spat.

"What does killing my father do for you? What does harming your best friend do? You got rid of your father, why keep doing this? Do you seriously need to kill dumb ass bullies just because you have a demon?" Ashton questioned. "Please.. Liam, don't let him kill my father.. I can't lose him," he whispered.

Liam watched Ashton for a moment before he shook his head. "I can't stop.. I don't know how. They tormented me in school, they do it outside of school, they do it all the time and they have to suffer for it!" He growled out. He narrowed his eyes once more and looked over at Stavros and Patrick. He watched the fighting, watched as Patrick would land a blow but Stavros remained standing and always seemed to land a harder blow.

"Someone will win this fight." Liam smirked.

Ashton felt his eye water again and he removed the belt wrapped around his head and the shirt "Liam." he whispered, looking up at him from his spot on his knees. "No one will win this fight." he whispered. He had five long gashes on the right side of his face, starting just below his hair line and ending just above his jaw going straight down, they barely missed Ashton' right eye. He knew Patrick or his father would win the fight they were having, but in the end did anyone really win the fight at all?

Liam looked at Ashton once again and blinked seeing the gashes on his face. He felt his heart break at the sight, he made that happen, he let that happen.. To his best friend. Who did such a thing to their best friend? "I..." he frowned and looked away. He felt confused, he was trying to work out what he should do. Did he want to stop this?

He knew how much pain Ashton would be in if he lost his father.. "Patrick.." he said softly, he knew the demon would hear him easily enough. "Stop. Don't kill him" he whispered. He looked at Ashton again with tears running down his face, "I'm so sorry.. I.. I don't know what came over me" he whispered.

Patrick was at Liam's side in an instant "What have you done?" he hissed at Ashton. "You've ruined what I was creating.. Now he's broken" he growled out. He was panting, the wounds were taking its toll on him but Patrick would need more than a few slashes or stab wounds to die. Stavros had a special blade that was made from demon bones but covered in some titanium for strength, it was one way to kill many demons but all demons had their own main weakness but the trick was trying to find it.

"I didn't ruin him.. I fixed him from what you were doing to him" Ashton snapped.

"You had your fun, now leave." Stavros, who was standing behind Ashton, hissed out. "Liam is no longer yours to control." he narrowed his eyes slowly.

Patrick laughed darkly, standing way too close to Liam for Ashton comfort, "True.. I had my fun and now it's over." he hissed. He smirked darkly and quickly spun on Liam, shoving his hand into Liam's chest and crushing his heart slowly, his body slowly healing as it devoured Liam's soul through his fingertips.

"NO! YOU SON OF A BITCH!" Ashton screamed. He jumped to his feet but Stavros was quick to wrap both arms around Ashton and pull him back to keep him away from the dangerous demon.

"Ashton there's nothing you can do!" he said loudly over Ashton' screaming and crying.

"NO! LET ME GO! Liam! Liam LOOK AT ME!" Ashton sobbed out.

Patrick laughed darkly and pulled his hand out of Liam's chest and smirked as the boys body dropped to the ground.

Ashton looked at his friend's lifeless body and everything around him blurred. He knew Patrick said something but honestly all he could do was scream, sob, and stare at his best friend's body. He tried yanking away from his father but he held onto him firmly.

His father finally released him when Patrick vanished like smoke into a breeze. Ashton stumbled over to Liam's body and sobbed as he dropped to his knees and pulled Liam's head onto his lap and held him tightly. He kept apologizing, wishing he had helped him better, wishing he did things differently, begging him to return but nothing worked. He sat there, cradling his best friend's head, sobbing. Everything around him was like white noise, he couldn't focus on anything, he heard his father murmur something but he had no idea what on earth he said but it seemed like moments later, Ashton was being pulled away from his best friends body. Ashton fought, tried staying with Liam, but the arms around him were like iron and refused to release him.

Stavros watched as Ashton sobbed over his best friends body, he had called the police, he knew they'd need to take the body. He walked over to Ashton "We need to back up." he murmured. He heard the sirens and knew the police would be here very soon. When Ashton didn't move at all, Stavros bent down and wrapped his arms around the boy and began to pry him away from Liam's body. He didn't care that Ashton fought, ignored his screams and sobs, as he continued to pull him back. He got Ashton onto his feet and held him close. He refused to release him, he just held him and whispered softly to him to try and sooth him.

The police arrived, tried speaking to Ashton but he couldn't say a word, he couldn't put what he happened into words, they eventually released him because Stavros gave his own statement on what had happened.

Ashton felt so numb by the end of it all, he couldn't cry anymore, couldn't think. He hardly noticed them taking Liam's body, hardly noticed being brought to the car and driven home. He barely even noticed Stavros speaking to him. Everything in the world was just faded, far away, just out of his reach but he couldn't care about that right now, the image of Liam's death replayed in his mind over and over again.

The next few days was such a blur, Liam's family gathered, they did the memorial, Ashton didn't speak at all then either. He hadn't spoken since they took Liam's body away from him. The day of the funeral was a blur as well, he remembered people saying words and Ashton had tried writing something down to say but he couldn't find his voice. This wasn't real, it couldn't be real, it was a huge nightmare and he needed to wake up but for some reason he couldn't. Ashton had nightmares of that day, had cried many times, and was still having a hard time believing it was even real.

Ashton was the last one standing by Liam's grave. He stared down at the coffin, he knew his father was beside him but also trying to give him space. For the first time since that day Ashton had started to think about everything else that had happened. He watched how his father fought against Tyler, how he killed him like it was nothing and even though Ashton knew his father got injured fighting Patrick, he had no wounds. Ashton' claw marks down his face had gotten stitches and still healing, though the doctor couldn't believe a cougar did it. Its what Stavros had to say because saying a human did it was unbelievable but a wild cat attack was the closest thing the scratch marks looked like it could be from, it couldn't be some human who did it. Human? No. Patrick and Tyler were not human. His father was not human.

Ashton stared down at the coffin and, for the first time since his best friend was killed, spoke to his father without looking at him. "What are you?" he whispered. His voice was hoarse from lack of use and from crying so much the last few days.

He heard his father sigh and take a few steps forward but then stopped, not wanting to get too close just yet. There was silence and Ashton was starting to think that he wouldn't get an answer but then his father spoke, he said one word and it made Ashton turn to stare at him in horror.

"Demon."

EPILOGUE

"I warned you all this was going to happen," a deep, angry, male voice growled out. The man sat in a dark room with four others. He had black shoulder length straight hair that had dark red tips and three days worth of beard on his chin. It was hard to judge his height with him sitting but he looked like he'd easily stand at 6' 7" and he had quite a bit of muscle on him. He wore no shirt, showing off a well formed six pack and tan skin all over his body. He did wear a black leather trench coat that was open and black jeans with black steel toe shoes. The room was dark with only a few candles to shine a little light around it. The table they sat at was red wood and long enough to fit at least twenty, and there were two servants in the room pouring red liquid into cups for those sitting at the table.

"Calm down, Killian. We all knew this was going to happen but the question now is, what are we going to do about it?" A female voice spoke. She had bright blue eyes and long blonde wavy hair that hung just below her butt. She stood by her chair, sipping her drink and wore a tight dark blue strapless dress that hugged every luscious curve of her 5' 6" body. She had on blue high heels that added another two inches to her height. She was a bit pale and skinny but not in an unhealthy way, it actually suited her hair and eyes perfectly. Her skin looked smooth and had no visible marking on it but even with her being thin she had muscle to her.

"That is why we are here, Rogue. We need to figure this stuff out. Lucian and Dakota couldn't make it here but they always seem to side with Stavros anyways," Jaded sighed. The man paced the room slowly holding his cup in his hand. He had short curly brown hair with dark brown eyes and dark skin. He stood at 6' 8" and wore a blood red shirt and blue jeans with black running shoes. He was a buffed up guy who looked like he could break anyone's neck with no issues. "We can't just kill him, nor do our powers fully affect him either," he muttered. It was a pity it worked like that. They could use their powers against each other but all eight of them knew how to battle against it. They all had at least two weaknesses but they had never trusted anyone enough to actually reveal what they were, because honestly, that was just a really stupid move.

Rogue rolled her eyes. "At one point we all sided with him but this is going over the line."

"How?" Killian rose a brow slowly. "Tyler and Patrick acted without permission from Stavros. He had a right to fight against them."

Jaded narrowed his eyes slowly. "If that is how you feel then why are you bitching about this?"

"Who said that was the issue I had?" Killian hissed.

"Alright. Fine. What *is* your issue then?" Rogue asked.

"What issue do I ever have with anyone?" Killian growled lowly. "He has that stupid little rodent living with him. It's disgusting. How can anyone be willing to put up with gross little things?" He shuddered. "It's foul and shouldn't be allowed. Even the live stock shouldn't be allowed to have those disgusting horrible shits but since they are our food, I allow it."

"Wait," Shadow chuckled. "You are here whining with these two idiots about Stavros, not because he killed Tyler, but because he has a child?" He laughed. Shadow was the tallest one in the room at 6' 9". He had blood red eyes, pale skin, and straight black hair with gray and white streaks in it that touched the bottom of his chin. He had a red dragon tattoo around his right eye, the tail ended just beside his lip and the body went around the eye and ended with the head above his right brow. He had long red fingernails that looked sharp enough to pierce through metal. He wore a black silk shirt with black dress pants and nothing on his feet. He didn't like how shoes or socks felt on his feet so he hardly ever wore them.

"Shut your mouth, Shadow," Killian barked out. "Children are horrible little things that really shouldn't be around at all."

Shadow grinned, showing off two long fangs with two smaller fangs right beside them. "I really hope one day you decided to actually bang someone and have a child because seeing how you'd raise one of those 'disgusting horrible shits' would be highly amusing. I swear people would pay millions just to watch you with that child for an hour," he joked with a laugh.

Killian gagged. "I'd never have one! And I've had sex many times." His voice was a snarl.

"Two times does not count as 'many,'" Rogue said with a soft giggle.

Killian shot to his feet and glared at her. "Now both of you shut up!" He snapped. "My sex life isn't what we are here to talk about."

"Or lack thereof..." Jaded muttered. Shadow almost dropped his drink from how hard he laughed at Killian's face.

Killian hissed at Jaded and went to lunge at him but Shadow moved fast and pinned the angry demon Lord down into his chair. "There is no fighting here, Killian," Shadow pointed out.

"I'm surprised you were willing to actually touch him to stop him." Jaded said. He and Shadow never got along all that great.

"Well it's not like I'm going to get any sexual diseases from him," Shadow said with a smirk. He moved away from Killian just as the man swung to punch him. Shadow tsked. "Now now, behave child or I'll have to give you a spanking."

Killian growled deep in his throat. "I hate all of you."

Shadow just gave a laugh. "Can you name anyone you *don't* hate?" He asked. "Exactly," he added, when Killian just looked away and said nothing.

Tabitha, the fifth person in the room, slammed a fist on the table for attention so she could sign. Tabitha had ash curly hair that went down to her shoulder blades and dark green eyes. Her skin was soft but covered in scars from so many different weapons that she didn't even know what they were all from anymore. She never paid attention to those things, she didn't care about having scars because it showed she was a fighter and survived her battles. She was tan and the shortest one standing at 5' 4" and was thin. Most of them stayed thin and well muscled because of how often they fought in some form of battle. She wore a white tank top and blue jeans with flats.

"All of you shut up and actually think about what we are going to do. We can't kill Stavros," she signed, once they all looked at her. Tabitha could speak, but she hated talking because her tongue had been badly burned when she was younger and it hurt to speak.

Jaded groaned some. "We know that," he sighed heavily. He rubbed his temples and glared at the four there. "So, any great ideas?"

Shadow shrugged slightly. "I honestly don't care. You four can come up with some stupid plan but leave me out of whatever it is because I already know you guys will mess it all up." They were idiots when it came to planning anything together because all they did was fight over it, and when the time actually came to doing what they planned they always refused to work together and decided to do their own little plans.

"Then why are you even here?" Killian asked. "You already knew what we'd be talking about so why waste our time having to listen to your useless words?" he growled.

Shadow smiled. "Oh baby, you know I could never stay away from you too long." He winked which succeeded in pissing Killian off.

"You are disgusting," Killian snarled. His face was a mask of disgust as he glared at Shadow.

"You keep talking like that and I'll kick all these losers out just so I can really show you how much I've missed you," Shadow purred. He licked his lips and looked Killian over slowly. "I'm so glad you decided to come here shirtless. Maybe next time I'll be real lucky and you'll end up forgetting your pants, or, better yet, you'll arrive naked." Shadow shivered with joy at the thought.

Killian felt like he was going to throw up. "Sorry, disgusting filth, you aren't my type."

Shadow snorted. "I didn't think you had a type, since you don't have sex."

"If we weren't in your domain I would be ripping you to shreds!" Killian snarled. Shadow gave a slow grin.

"Are sure you don't mean you'd shred my clothes?"

"Enough!" Rogue snapped. "We are getting nowhere with you two going on like this. Focus!" She crossed her arms over her chest.

Shadow rolled his eyes. "Someone likes to ruin my fun. Whatever, you guys keep talking. Next time go to someone else's place okay?" Their meeting room was in Shadow's basement because he could use the shadows to block out everywhere outside of the room and he could also use his shadows to keep someone pinned if they tried attacking someone. Shadow's powers were the only ones that could work on all of them to an extent.

Tabitha hit the table again. *"You fool. If you have nothing to say that would be helpful, sit down and shut up."*

Jaded mumbled to himself about being stuck with useless children. He cleared his throat and spoke. "We are here to discuss Stavros. He has grown soft over the years because of that boy he has. How can he call himself a demon Lord if he can't even act like one? He acts like a human and we can't allow that."

"Is it really that bad?" Shadow asked with a sigh. "The boy will die at some point and Stavros will return to himself when that happens. Humans only live for a handful of years, that's nothing compared to the millions of centuries we live."

"None of us are that old," Killian snorted. "And even if the gross thing does die, Stavros is attached to it now and it's not like he'll go back to how he used to be when it does. We can't sit around and wait for that to happen."

"Exactly." Rogue chimed in. "It needs to be handled soon or else it'll mess everything up."

"Everything?" Shadow asked. He rose a brow slowly as he looked at her. "What do we have planned exactly? Because last time I checked we are demons with very simple minds. All we seem to care about is our next meal, fun sexy times, ruling over other demons and fucking shit up. None of that involves actually planning anything and if you do have to plan it then you are just a terrible demon who really shouldn't be lord of anything." His vice was a soft growl as he spoke.

Rogue glared at Shadow and flipped him off. "That may be your plan but the rest of us would like to do a lot more with our lives."

"You mean our never ending life?" Shadow asked. "We've been alive for a really long time and have only planned the wars, which didn't take much planning. Humans are greedy little assholes and are so simple to control or push into destroying each other. We are demons they don't even know about, and they sure as hell don't know we pull all their strings. Humans are needy, greedy, cowardly, little pests. Really, the list could go on and on about what they are and, sadly, with how you guys are freaking out about this shit, it just makes you sound like whiny little humans." He liked demons as much as he liked humans and he couldn't stand humans. He didn't need souls like the rest of them, even though he did feed on them when he was bored.

Rogue growled low in her throat but before she could say anything Jaded spoke.

"Both of you knock it off. Yes, Shadow, we all know how you feel about all this, and at times I do agree that some of us sound like whiny humans, but this is a serious matter so at least act like it. Like damn, I know we can't stand to be around each other but at least act grown up long enough for us to finish this conversation so we can just leave." His voice was stern, and he'd hit them all over the head if he could, but he knew that it would just start another fight and he really just wanted to get this over with so he could leave.

Shadow grumbled some curses to himself but said nothing more as he sat in his chair and played around with his cup.

Killian sighed heavily. "As it has been pointed out, we can't kill Stavros." He glanced around at them. "We do not know his normal weaknesses but he does have one that he hadn't planned on having," he said.

Rogue tilted her head curiously. "Oh? And what exactly is that?"

Tabitha shook her head slowly. "*I know where you are going with this, Killian, and it isn't a good idea.*" She signed.

"Why not?" Killian asked. "You guys wanted to solve this problem and we have a way to do it."

"*No,*" Tabitha signed. "*You have a way for him to want war against all of us.*"

Killian gave a small smirk. "You are talking to the Lord of war, dumbass. I'd be more than happy to start one with him." He always did enjoy a good war, especially against a powerful opponent. He liked when his wars went on for years and he knew Rogue loved it since she was the Lord of destruction.

"What is it?" Rogue barked out. She hated when they did this. Why couldn't they share the full plan first and then argue about whether it was a good idea or not?

Killian smirked again as he sat back in his chair and looked at them all. "Ashton," he growled. "He raised that boy for ten years and has grown attached to it. It has made Stavros soft which isn't good for us. We need to remove Ashton so Stavros can return to us."

Shadow snorted but remained silent. He knew it was a stupid idea and he wasn't about to have a part in it.

"You'd never get Dakota or Lucian to agree," Jaded pointed out.

"Or Shadow." Shadow spoke for himself.

"Or Shadow," Jaded added, rolling his eyes. "If you are going to try getting that boy away from Stavros we all need to work together."

"No, we don't." Killian said. He sighed and shook his head slowly. "The pest goes to school and he does leave Stavros' sight so we can do it when he's alone." He gave a shrug.

"What are we suppose to do with him?" Rogue asked. "It's not like we can just lock him up somewhere and hope Stavros never finds him again. Stavros will tear the world apart to find him." She sighed. This was giving her a headache and she really wished she had blown this meeting off.

Killian growled as he slowly stood. "Are you completely brain dead? Like honestly, do you know how to think? Or even follow a conversation?"

"It's not my fault you don't give all the information right away," Rogue snapped at him. "Please, oh great know-it-all, what is the plan? Where would you keep him? What would we do with him?"

Tabitha rolled her eyes and watched as Jaded continued to pace. They were idiots and how she had managed to stay here without trying to rip someone's throat out was amazing.

Killian ran his fingers through his hair and took a sip of his drink. He licked his lips and gave Rogue a hard look. "To put things into simple words for you, simple minded female, we wouldn't keep it anywhere."

"Than where-"

"We will kill him." Killian cut her off. He smirked and slowly wiped the blood from his bottom lip with his thumb. "We will punish Stavros by killing Ashton."

CPSIA information can be obtained
at www.ICGtesting.com
Printed in the USA
BVHW031152011119
562694BV00001B/108/P